Queen Victoria's Revenge

by HARRY HARRISON

Queen Victoria's Revenge

HARRY HARRISON

PUBLISHED FOR THE CRIME CLUB BY
DOUBLEDAY & COMPANY, INC.
GARDEN CITY, NEW YORK
1974

All of the characters in this book are fictitious, and any resemblance to actual persons, living or dead, is purely coincidental.

Library of Congress Cataloging in Publication Data

Harrison, Harry.
    Queen Victoria's revenge.

    I. Title.
PZ4.H319Qe [PS3558.A667] 813'.5'4
ISBN 0-385-07802-1
Library of Congress Catalog Card Number 73-81435

for Tony's godfather
LARRY ASHMEAD

ONE

Forty-five thousand feet above the surface of the earth the sky is clear dark blue, a world of emptiness between outer space and the white blanket of the clouds far below. The air here is far too thin for any creature to breathe, but is solid enough substance for the gaping mouths of jet engines. This is their realm, great silver craft such as the DC-10 that now hurtled into visibility, streaking through the rarefied atmosphere at six hundred miles an hour, arching over the landscape of North America eight and a half miles below. A new leviathan of the skies with an immense single tail that rose almost sixty feet above the fuselage and supported the bulky cylinder of a giant engine. The insignia above the engine was the proud red crescent and star of Moslem, accompanied by the delicate curls and twists of an Arabic inscription. For the benefit of the unbeliever, and to conform to the exigencies of international law, the message was translated lower on the tail in roman lettering.

AIR MECCA it read, and these same words were spelled out on both sides of the fuselage.

No sound could possibly be heard through the airtight walls of the great airship, soundproofed to cut out the roar of the three immense turbo fan engines, and the sounds inside were weak enough. Some screams, wails of fear, guttural curses. Harsh commands were issued, backed by the authority of the gun barrel, until with some reluctance they were obeyed. The instructions were printed on paper and very clear.

With ponderous ease the plane tilted up on one wing and executed a slow turn, then settled onto its new course. Invisible radio messages crackled from its antenna.

"No," Tony Hawkin said into the mouthpiece of the telephone in response to the syrupy voice that cajoled in his ear. "No, I don't really think we could possibly be interested in chocolate handcuffs. Yes, I do know that the chocolate bullets have been a solid selling line, but bullets are, you know, meant to be expended. An edible handcuff seems to be a contradiction in itself. Yes, good-bye."

Hanging up, he surveyed his little kingdom with a professional eye. The book and souvenir shop of the Federal Bureau of Investigation appropriately located in the lobby of the FBI Building in Washington, D.C., was doing its normal trade. Small children and their larger parents were pawing over and buying items from his irresistible collection of toy fingerprint sets, gilt badges, black-framed photographs of the former director, books of great crimes (solved) and photographs of master criminals (apprehended). His two assistants bustled and wrapped while the merry chime of the cash register sang its golden song. It was a scene that should have filled any shopkeeper's heart with joy—yet why was he frowning? Thin and of medium height, neatly but not showily dressed as the Bureau commanded, tanned and black-haired and not unattractive, his nose perhaps a little on the large size, he was a fine figure of a man at ease in his own domain. Still the acid dripped steadily in his vitals and he was sure that if he did not already have an ulcer one was just around the corner. For although his body was in this stronghold of law enforcement his soul was still in the National Gallery. Not by choice had he been parted from his Degas and Da Vincis, Turners and Tiepolos, but by the force of draft. Circumstance had plucked him from the world of art and transformed him into an inadvertent and most reluctant lawman. Despite the success and adulation of his newfound calling his single, burning wish remained steadfast: he wanted out. The acid dripped and the ulcer twinged.

A forceful movement caught his eye. Two stern-faced and soberly dressed men, in step, were plowing a straight path through the aimless millings of the tourists. This was not an uncommon occurrence for, in addition to giving guided tours and providing material for television programs, the Bureau still had a positive role in national law enforcement. Agents came and agents went and none was to say where and why. Which was fine with Tony—the less he knew about the operations of the Bureau the happier he was—except these two agents seemed to have their steely gaze firmly planted on *him*.

Unerringly they approached and, with each doomlike footstep, Tony's heart sank a bit more. Memories of previous forced employment unreeled before him: a knife between dead shoulder blades, beatings, screams in the night, hurried journeys and ugly violence. Not again! Yet even as he breathed the wish he knew it was a vain one. Thudding footsteps came close and stopped, solid blue jaws leaned near. A breath redolent of mint and Bianca, empty of alcohol or tobacco, breathed in his ear.

"Top priority emergency, Agent Hawkin. Come with us."

This last was more a courtesy than a request for, even while the agent was talking, strong hands were laid on Tony's arm in some complicated manner that appeared to be a friendly clutch while in reality was an iron embrace that lifted and propelled him along between the matched pair. He made paddling motions with his feet so his toes would not drag and scuff his shine.

In an instant they were out of the lobby and a moment later down a long hall. Doors opened before them and closed behind them, an elevator lifted them skyward and more doors greeted them until their journey ended in a spacious office before a large desk behind a door labeled simply 2135. The two guides departed without a word and Tony brushed the wrinkles from his sleeve. "I think there has been a mistake," he said.

"So do I, Hawkin," Ross Sones said. "So do I. I know you did well on Operation Buttercup, but I don't really think this is your piece of cake."

"Agreed. See you around, Ross."

"However," Sones said, and the authority in his voice stopped Tony as he was turning away, spun him about and dropped him into the waiting chair, "however, orders are orders. And these are right from the computer." He tapped the accordion folds of computer readout on the desk as though they were sacred scripture, his head lowered with reverence. The three strands of thin hair pasted across the bald expanse of his skull served only as reminders of their long-vanished brethren. With his beady eyes, pimp's hairline mustache, thin nose and gold-rimmed pince-nez glasses he looked the part of a failed confidence man. Tony knew him to be a humorless and highly efficient FBI agent.

"Orders for what?" Tony said, dully. Like a rabbit in the noose he had abandoned all hope of salvation. Sones ignored the interruption.

"Request came through, secret and urgent, for an agent with certain qualifications. You were the only name the computer produced."

Tony hated the gross bulk of the omniscient machine. "Can't you tell it I have ulcers and ask for the runner-up? What are the qualifications?"

"That information is classified." A deep buzzing sounded from his desk as though a giant captive bee were calling for release. "There's the signal. We go in now."

The conference room was brightly lit, humming with activity, shrill with ringing phones. Most of the action was centered on the long table where a number of men were doing interesting things with a great deal of money. This was being unloaded, a bundle at a time, from a large suitcase at the far end, where every grasping hand moved under the piercing and unblinking gaze of a big man in a lumpy brown suit.

"Hello, Stocker," Tony said as he passed and was answered by a suspicious quick look from under the beetling brows of the Treasury agent.

"Ah hope yore not involved in this affair, Hawkin." His voice was hard as tool steel. "Still that matter of a hundred dollars from Mexico . . ."

"Well if everyone is so wildly enthusiastic about having me there will be no problem with my leaving."

"Hawkin, here."

The command was crisp, the voice used to authority. This was the top agent Tony knew only as X, the man who had involved him with the almost catastrophic Mexican affair. He now appeared to be in charge of the present operation—whatever it was—and Tony hurried over in response to the command, resisting the urge to come to attention and salute, this reflex rising from the depths of his brain where it had been drilled in during his term of involuntary service in the Army.

"Sir?"

"Take off your shoes."

Carried away by the current of events, he sat dumbly and did as he had been ordered, with the unquestioning obedience of any Watergate conspirator. His shoes were whisked away. X shook a computer printout accusingly.

"We needed an agent with specific attributes and yours was the only name produced." Still the same wild enthusiasm for Tony's participation.

"I'm sure another agent could be found who would be more qualified," Tony said, smiling hopefully.

"That's not what the computer thinks. I need an agent who can speak Spanish and is familiar with handling large sums of money . . ."

"There must be lots of those."

". . . and who is in this building now. Do you know what this is?" He handed Tony a glossy photograph of a large airplane.

"It is a glossy photograph of a large airplane."

"That is obvious." X's voice was blurred since, for some reason, he was speaking with his teeth clamped tightly together. "I mean what *kind* of an aircraft."

"Passenger?" Tony said hopefully and the clamped teeth ground slowly from side to side.

"Sones. Get the intelligence report and see that he is completely briefed on the DC-10 before he leaves."

"It's a DC-10," Tony said, but was ignored. X tapped the photograph with a hard finger.

"One of these was skyjacked five hours ago. It will be coming in to Dulles in about half an hour. There is a ransom to be paid." Tony started to ask something about shooting out tires then, wisely, refrained. "We know ransom isn't the answer in most cases but this one has both political and religious overtones." Apparently satisfied with these gnostic statements he turned his attention back to the table, pausing only to throw an afterthought over his shoulder. "You'll be boarding the money." With little formality Sones pulled Tony aside and rustled a sheaf of papers.

"The DC-10 has three General Electric CF6-6D turbo fan engines each putting out forty thousand pounds of thrust. It seats . . ."

"Sones! The plane later. Would you mind telling me first about these political and religious overtones? I have a feeling I should know."

Sones pondered this, taking off his glasses and polishing them, while frowning deeply to help the pondering. A conclusion was reached.

"This plane is named the Hadji and is owned by Air Mecca. This is a Mideast carrier that specializes in ferrying pilgrims to Mecca, the holiest city of Islam in Saudi Arabia, fifty miles from the port of Jidda. Up until now it has been a small operation using war-weary C-47's. However it has expanded and purchased this jumbo jet. The Hadji, with two hundred and eighty-three pilgrims from Asia, landed for refueling at Los Angeles. The passengers were disembarked for this. They reboarded and the plane started for the next stop for passengers in Dakar, before proceeding to Mecca. However it appears that an unknown number of skyjackers boarded with the pilgrims and have now seized the plane. They threaten to destroy it and all the passengers, and themselves, of course, if they do not immediately receive two million dollars. We are marking the money now."

Tony let this rather startling information sink in for a moment until one glaring inconsistency surfaced.

"Well that's all very nice—but what has the speaking of Spanish to do with Arabs and Moslems?"

"Nothing. But the skyjackers speak only Spanish. They are anti-Castro Cubans."

Any expected, or unexpected, answer to this was pre-empted by the arrival of a great gaunt old man with a mean cast in his eye and Tony's shoes in his hand. The curl of his lip assured another enthusiastic acceptance of Tony's presence. Old Fred, the FBI weapons specialist, had never taken kindly to Tony.

"You are not going to be armed, blast it, which is probably all for the best, considering . . ." A world of statement lurked behind the last word, memories of Tony on the firing range, guns dropped, targets missed, eyes closed. "But these shoes may make a difference. The right heel is resealed in place and contains a radio with a transmitting range of a quarter of a mile and a battery life of twenty hours. The microphone is here on the side—see it?—keep your blasted fingers off it. Try not to move your feet when you're talking to those crumbbums so we can monitor your conversation. Now, the other shoe—on this one the blasted left heel pivots from the rear like this and contains seven small grenades, see them? *Don't* take them out, blast it! One of them could blow up this entire room. Put the shoes on. This is a dummy of one of the grenades, you will see it is labeled *dummy* in yellow. To activate this blasted grenade you pull up on this pin here and then you throw it because it explodes three seconds after the pin is pulled. Is that all clear?"

"Very," Tony said coldly and bent to put his shoes back on, more than a little tired of the general assumption that his intelligence and ability fell somewhere between a microcephalic idiot and a spastic basket case. After all he was an art historian—it was their idea to call him an FBI agent. He was probably the only person in the room who had ever heard of the Mannerists or knew something more about Van Gogh than the fact he had cut his ear off. This reassurance helped not in the slightest.

"Don't stamp your blasted heel too much. Them grenades can be tricky sometimes." As he spoke this morale-building advice Old Fred produced a snub-nosed revolver in a quick-draw holster, neatly imprinted with the initials FBI, which he fitted into place on Tony's belt.

"What's this? What's this? A minute ago you said I wasn't going to be armed. Are they supposed to think this is a carbuncle on my hip?"

"Blasted skyjackers expect an agent to be armed. They'll search you and find this."

"Very generous of the FBI to turn over dangerous weapons to known criminals."

"Nope. Gun's rigged to explode if anyone tries to fire it. And if they really search you they'll find this. Should satisfy them."

This was what appeared to be a length of thick wire that had been looped at each end. Old Fred quickly wrapped it around Tony's wrist and taped it into place, then slid his watch back down to cover its presence.

"Gigli saw," he explained. "Used in brain surgery for sawing out hunks of skull. Got notches in it like teeth. Blasted tough. Can saw bars or be used as a garrote to choke someone. Blasted handy."

"Just what I have always needed. Is that all?"

"All from me."

"The DC-10 has a cruising speed of six hundred miles an hour . . ."

"Sones, please, a little less airplane and a little more information on the skyjacking. How did they manage this thing with all the precautions we are supposed to have?"

"The details are not completely clear. The passengers deplaned in Los Angeles while the plane was refueling. There are a lot of them and I understand the transit lounge was pretty full. Also they were dressed in an unusual manner, you know, robes and things. It appears the skyjackers were similarly dressed and just boarded with the crowd."

"Weapons too?"

"Plenty of them. They made the captain describe their arms. Pistols, submachine guns, grenades, satchel charges, bayonets."

"No anti-tank guns?"

"None were reported."

"I'm surprised. They seem to have gotten everything else they needed aboard."

"There will be an investigation."

"Which won't help me in the slightest. So this small army is aboard and makes its presence known after they take off. How many of them are there?"

"Captain Haycroft, the plane's commander, reported twelve. They seized control of the ship and diverted to Dulles Airport here in Washington. They also asked for the two million dollars to be waiting when they landed. They threatened to kill one passenger a minute for every minute they had to wait for the money. After sixty minutes, or sixty passengers, they will blow the entire plane up. The money has been provided." He waved in the direction of the long table where the industrious agents were still stamping the bills with invisible identification of many kinds.

"I should hope so. Who put up the cash?"

"Treasury is providing the cash. But there were some quick phone calls and ten of the Arab countries, the oil ones of course, have guaranteed two hundred thousand dollars each."

"Then what?"

"When the money is aboard they agree to release most of the hostages. They want the plane refueled and after takeoff will announce their destination. The plane has a wingspan of one hundred and fifty-five feet, four inches . . ."

"Hawkin, let's go." X's voice cut through the murmur of the room and pulled Tony to his feet as though he had been jerked by a rope. The head agent stood scowling down at the repacked suitcase, agleam with mint-fresh greenies. "We have used radioactive marking so these bills can be detected by a geiger counter or similar device. Under black light the legend SKYJACKED CURRENCY is revealed. The right-hand edge of every bill is coated with a saccharin solution very sweet to the tongue. And— *Buenos días, señor Hawkin. Como está usted?*"

He looked up at Tony and waited expectantly. Tony blinked

and ran the sentence through his mind a few times until he finally understood that it was badly pronounced high school Spanish which, with some effort, he translated.

"*Ah, sí, me siento muy bien gracias y espero que te sientas igual. Que español tan perfecto hablas. ¿Porque no vas al avion . . . ?*"

"That sounds all right, Hawkin. But the files do not explain how you, an American Indian, came to speak a foreign language so well."

"If you will look closer at the record you will see that I grew up in Palm City, California, on the Mexican border, where Spanish is not only not a foreign language but the language of choice for most of the population."

X frowned and chewed over this fact and eventually accepted it. He gestured to the big Treasury agent, Stocker, who still hovered over the money like an eagle guarding its kill. Stocker swooped and slammed the bag shut and locked it. He also clamped a handcuff around Tony's right wrist and locked that as well; the cuff was secured to the handle of the bag. Both keys were in a small key case, which, with some show of reluctance, he finally handed to Tony.

"Yore responsible fur this two million dollars, Hawkin. Treasury is still fussin' over that hundred dollars you . . ."

"Just the keys if you please, Stocker. Thanks." He put them in his pocket. "If you want a quick course in Spanish you can have the money back."

"Here we go, Hawkin, on your toes. The plane is in the landing pattern."

Sones and another burly agent flanked him and started him toward the door. And he really was on his toes, as much as possible, painfully aware of the heel-load of explosive.

TWO

Tony had always wanted to travel this way, however he wished that the circumstances were different so that he could have enjoyed it more. A large black Cadillac, doors gaping, was waiting at the curb outside. Motorcyclists surrounded it, exhausts hammering, while police cars waited back and front. There was even an army half-track, filled with heavily armed troops, to bring up the tail of the convoy. All was in readiness. The instant the doors closed, before they were even seated, the car shot forward. Roaring with power, the motorcycles matched their velocity and the impressive group of vehicles tore down the broad avenue.

Apparently other police units had gone ahead and stopped all traffic, for they moved at a steady sixty miles an hour through the city. Once they were on the highway this whooshed up to a good hundred miles an hour and the half-track was forced to drop behind, shrinking to an olive drab speck before it vanished behind a turn. They hurled themselves through the green Virginia countryside and into the turnoff for Dulles International Airport. Above them, bulking large against the blue afternoon sky, was the hovering hulk of an airplane that Tony, now, recognized as a DC-10.

"Is that it?" he asked Sones, who was in the front seat muttering into a microphone, headphones clamped to head.

"It is. The tower had them in the stack as long as possible but they insisted on landing. Can't argue. This is going to be a close-run thing. We'll have to stay out of the terminal and go directly onto the field."

It took a good deal of firm persuasion, and some calling in of higher authorities, to convince the airport authorities that the car should be allowed out among the runways. The outriders and police cars peeled off at the gate so that the Cadillac shot through in solitary splendor. All other traffic was halted as they sped toward the boarding area in the center of the field, their arrival coinciding with that of the Hadji DC-10, which was just turning off the taxiway.

There are certain interesting facts about Dulles Airport that must be considered, other than its being named in memory of that stern architect of the cold war. For particular reasons, some financial, others physical, planes do not pull up to the terminal as they do in other airports around the world. Instead the planes wait expectantly a good half mile from the cant-roofed, glass-walled terminal building. The departing passengers, all unknowing, exit through gates in the normal manner, surrendering passes, being frisked, and board beyond the gate what must be the ugliest vehicle ever to be powered by an internal combustion engine.

This is a people transporter. A sort of railroad coach body standing high in the air on hydraulic pistons. Far below is the supporting structure borne on great rubber tires. Once loaded, the vehicle backs out and squats like a collapsing praying mantis, both at the same time. Roughly at ground level, it drives to the waiting plane at a majestic twelve miles an hour, where, hydraulically once again, the passenger section rises a good eighteen feet into the air to align with the plane's doorway.

One of these constructions was already lumbering its way toward the arriving plane. The FBI car passed it and stopped, waiting with throbbing impatience. A meet was accomplished; the DC-10 shuddered and braked while the whistling roar of its great engines died away. The transporter arrived. Tony was hustled to its door, pushed through in lonely solitude, to sit and clutch the money bag to his bosom as the body rose under the deft manipulation of the driver-operator who sat in the glassed-in nose. The operator mated the open end against the plane's hull with the door centered neatly. After a brief hesitation the door moved inward and upward an inch and stopped. A deep voice spoke through the opening:

"*El chofer se irá detras del camión, lo más lejos posible.*"

"He wants you in the back," Tony told the gray-haired and unhappy driver. "As far back as you can get."

"He doesn't have to say it twice." The man moved quite swiftly.

"*Está bien, ya se fué el chofer,*" Tony said, and a moment later the door opened a bit wider to reveal a suspicious eye and the muzzle of a machine gun.

"Are you alone?"

"Of course." Tony tried to sound firm and determined but his voice had a certain tendency to crack. Not without reason, he thought, gloomily.

"You have the money, all of it?"

"In here." He shook the bag in the direction of the eye and tried to ignore the gun. The door moved up and inward and vanished from sight. A hulking, brown-skinned man rose from his knees and waved Tony forward with a sharp motion of the submachine gun that he was holding in an efficient-looking manner. Tony entered.

It was a scene out of *Lawrence of Arabia,* lacking only a blown-up railroad and a couple of horses. The Spanish-speaking gunman wore an Arab burnoose with crossed cartridge belts, as did a half-dozen gun-wielding companions. Some of them even had part of the cloth drawn over their faces so that only glittering and deadly eyes remained revealed. Beyond them, to complete the picture, was row after row of similarly garbed men and women, eyes damp with fear, the air rich with moans of despair, the deck thick with prayer rugs being industriously prayed upon, hopefully in the direction of Mecca, their elusive goal.

"On the deck and open it up."

Tony's attention was brought rudely back from this fascinating scene to the business at hand. He reached in his pocket for his keys and six gun barrels pointed unerringly at his vitals while ugly fingers twitched at triggers.

"The keys," he said sweatingly, "I need the keys for the bag and the handcuff."

"Just pose in that position for a little-little moment while I get the keys and whatever else you have."

The burly speaker, apparently their leader, cold of eye and grizzled of hair, swung the machine gun over his shoulder and gave Tony a quick and efficient search. He was not surprised to find the revolver, and stuck it and the holster into his belt, but discovered nothing else to interest him other than the keys. He tossed them to Tony, who opened both locks, then knelt and opened the bag upon the deck.

Even the faithful were interested in two million dollars in devalued American currency and there were murmurs of appreciation in a number of languages. The leader pushed Tony aside roughly and knelt in his stead, pawing through the bundles, counting the bills in a bundle and then the number of bundles. All must have been in order, for he nodded approval and snapped the bag shut again.

"It is here, boys, all of it."

There were one or two enthusiastic shouts that quickly died away and it was back to business again.

"Hold this," the leader said, thrusting the bag once more into Tony's reluctant arms. "Up forward with it—you go with him, Jorge. Put him in the flight deck. Let's move these people out."

Urged on by the prodding muzzle of Jorge's pistol, Tony worked his way forward through the ebb and surge of burnoosed figures. Moist dark eyes stared with fright in his direction, birdlike voices tremoloed incomprehensible remarks. The gun moved him on. At the far end of the cabin a brace of rest rooms framed the door to the flight deck. Two more of the Cuban-Arabs guarded the doorway, a study in contrasts. The one on the right, to whom Jorge was talking, was a small man with tiny feet. His companion stood well over six feet tall and had shoes like canal boats. A turn of cloth covered most of his face, just revealing the blue eyes set in a patch of dark skin.

"In here," Jorge ordered, opening the door.

As soon as he did this things became very busy very quickly. A handful of red-uniformed men waiting inside struggled for an instant in the doorway, then burst through and fell upon the skyjackers. They were armed with an assortment of tools, hammers and wrenches, and gained an upper hand by the suddenness of their attack. Two of the Cubans were instantly on the deck, overwhelmed, while strong hands tore at their weapons. It might have ended there except for the intervention of the tall skyjacker. He had taken his own attacker out at once with an arm across the throat, followed instantly by a knee in the belly. Even as the wrench was falling from limp fingers, and the unconscious figure dropping toward the deck, his assailant was moving on. With the butt of his gun he caught one man a wicked blow in the skull, turning instantly to kick the other under the chin. Before Tony could move or even think of taking a role in the brief and nasty encounter, it was over, the massive survivor swinging his weapon obnoxiously over the heaped and groaning bodies, turning toward Tony expectantly as though looking forward to polishing him off as a final course.

"*Como puede ver, yo no estóy haciendo nada, nomas estóy viendo,*" Tony said, smiling hopefully and clutching the bag of money to his chest. Further than ever from his beloved Braques and Breughels. The skyjacker leaned forward, as though intent upon a little additional mayhem, but stopped when there were angry shouts, and pained screams, as two more of the skyjackers pushed through the crowd of passengers. The gray-haired man, apparently the leader, took in the situation at a glance and sorted it out with sharp orders. The three uniformed attackers, obviously the flight crew, were pushed, groaning or inert, back into the flight deck along with Tony and his suitcase of money. A guard entered with them and stood with his back to the closed door, the twitching muzzle of his submachine gun menacing them all.

"Tengo ordenes de matar a cualquiera persona que me de molestias," he said with snarling sincerity.

"Te creemos, te creemos," Tony answered, putting down the money and turning to the groaning survivors. The nearest one, a chubby pink man with thinning hair, opened one bloodshot eye and moaned horribly.

"He says he'll kill anyone who tries this again," Tony said brightly.

"Don't need a translator for that, buddy." He touched his jaw and examined his palm gloomily for traces of blood. "Who are you?"

"Tony Hawkin of the FBI." Said that way it sounded very impressive.

"Well *good* for you. I'm John Waterbury, copilot. Is that the ransom money?"

"Yes."

"Thanks for small blessings. Those nuts were ready to kill us or I wouldn't have let the captain talk us into trying to crack out of here. Here, help me with him, he doesn't look so good. Waldo, get the first-aid kit."

The flight engineer, Waldo, a thin and gloomy man—who now had good reason to be gloomy, if not thin—pulled out the box under the watchful eye of their guard. "Looks pretty sick to me, Tubby," he said.

Waterbury must have been used to the nickname for he made no protest but quickly, and efficiently, attended to the unconscious pilot on the deck. The captain was a burly, middle-aged man with the build of an ex-football player. He lay, breathing hoarsely, with blood running from a nasty-looking wound in his scalp. Tubby quickly swabbed and applied a padded bandage, then wrapped it in place with lengths of gauze. When he had done he cracked a glass cylinder of ammonium carbonate under his nose. The captain's nostrils twitched under the attack of the pungent ammonia fumes and his eyes snapped open. He looked around at all present, then fixed his gaze on Tony, the downed tackle ready to play again.

"I am Captain Sterling Haycroft in charge of this aircraft. Who are you?"

"Hawkin of the FBI. I've brought the money."

"We were concerned that they might not come through. These are very desperate men."

"That must have been realized or the money would not have been rounded up so quickly."

"Does that gorilla behind you speak English?" Haycroft spoke in the same tone of voice, not looking at the guard.

"I have no idea."

"It would be nice to know. Watch him, Tubby, and let me know if he twitches or changes expression because I am going out of here in a minute and report to the head skyjacker that this thug not only looks like Castro but he is a well-known pansy communist and sexual pervert hated by all animal lovers in the civilized world."

"The FBI has him in their dangerous communist files," Tony added enthusiastically, "and the ASPCA is also keeping a close watch on him."

"Let's not overdo it, Hawkin. Tubby?"

"He twitched a bit when you mentioned the name of you-know-who, but other than that he looks pretty bored. He's been picking his nose and shows more interest in his treasures than the conversation. I have a feeling that he either does not speak English or is the world's greatest actor."

"We'll take it as operational for the moment that he doesn't. Can you tell us what is happening, Hawkin? Everything on the radio has been in Spanish, then they pulled one of the radio circuits after we landed. All we know is that we were cleared for landing here at Dulles and if a ransom wasn't delivered upon arrival we would be shot. Nothing else."

"I have it here," he patted the suitcase. "Two million in fresh greenbacks. They are disembarking the passengers now and—I'm sorry to say this—they will keep holding the crew as hostages."

Haycroft nodded unsmilingly. "We didn't expect anything

different. At least the passengers are being off-loaded. I see the
tanks are being filled—do you know our destination?"

"No, they haven't said a thing about that."

"All right. When you get back to the FBI tell them . . ."

His urgent message remained unspoken. The door opened
and a skyjacker poked his head in and jerked his thumb at Tony.

"*Venga aquí, policia, y no se le olvide lo contante sonante.*"
Tony grabbed up the bag hurriedly.

"I have to go. I'll report on the situation. I know they'll do
everything they can."

The flight crew did not appear overburdened with joy at this
information and their eyes followed him as he departed for free-
dom leaving them in continued confinement. The large cabins
were almost empty now; a clutter of orange skins, shawls and
an occasional slipper marked the sudden exit of the passengers.
The last of them were being forced, wailing, through the exit.
Wailing even louder were at least a dozen comely young women
in floor-length red and white gowns who clutched to each other
in the rear of the center cabin under the watchful gun of a skyjacker. As the last passenger was ejected they screeched even
more shrilly, and pushed against the guard, driving him back.
He retreated before the onslaught and one of the girls, more
agile or more desperate than the others, took advantage of the
moment to leap gazelle-like over a row of seats and outflank him.
Holding her skirt knee-high, she ran past Tony, who had a quick
glimpse of an angry, yet lovely, face, churning, and equally attractive legs. She wore a red cap with golden wings and he
realized that the girls were all stewardesses, members of the
hostage crew. The escaping stewardess halted before the skyjackers at the entrance and pointed an accusing finger.

"Animals, you cannot do this! *Merde!* You . . . you *cretini*
cannot hold my girls, you hear! All good Moslem girls, not
ferengi koorvyenok like you! Let them go, no hostages zem!"

She had an admirable vocabulary in a number of languages,
though unhappily none of them was Spanish. The skyjackers
listened and nodded appreciatingly and made comments about

the fire in her eyes and her great spirit. It was their leader who tired of this first. He tore the suitcase of money away from Tony and jerked his thumb at the raging girl.

"*Dile que se calle y que se vuelva con los demas.*"

"Miss, please, listen to me . . ."

She spun about to face Tony, lovely in her anger, pushing a sprawl of raven hair from her eyes. "What eez eet? What does thees peeg say?"

"I'm sorry, but he wants you back with the other stewardesses. I'm afraid they are going to keep you all as hostages."

"Hostage?" She shouted the word in a rising scream and spun about again. "*Mandyee! Pastika misthaufen!*"

Words failed her, despite her fine command of many tongues, so she hooked her carmine-tipped fingers like a leopard's claws and hurled herself on the gray-haired skyjacker. The attack was so sudden that before he could defend himself her nails had raked great bloody furrows down his face. He roared with pain, lashing out. His pistol barrel caught her on the side of the temple and sent her sprawling back into a row of seats.

"That's the end!" he shouted, dancing with pain and dabbing at his face with the sleeve of his burnoose. "Get all of these bitches out of here, all of them, before I massacre them. I can't stand the sight of them. As long as we have the flight crew and this government agent they won't try any tricks."

"Not me!" Tony gasped. "I'm just a messenger."

"No trouble!" he shouted at Tony, shaking his pistol. "Just shut up and get ready for a nice long trip."

THREE

If profound despair can be said to be an overwhelming emotion, then Tony Hawkin was possessed by profound despair. The door was sealed once again and the interior of the great aircraft rang with happy Latin cries, which joy only depressed Tony the further. He was ignored, forgotten, not worth consideration. Bottles of rum appeared and were passed from mouth to dusty mouth. One of the bundles of hundred dollar bills was taken from the case and also passed around to be greatly admired. Weapons were shaken at the sight of it while there were joyous shouts of "*¡Viva la contra-revolución!*" It was almost unbearable. Not only that but Tony was thirsty too and needed a drink—perhaps even more than they did.

There was a water fountain next to the door to the flight deck. Tony went there and drank deep despite the fact the water had a musty, oriental quality. He would have preferred the rum. The rest room was close to hand and, still being ignored, he went in and locked the door and stared at himself in the mirror. He had looked better. In a feeble attempt at morale building he washed his hands and face in cold water, then combed his hair and applied some skin bracer from a bottle on the counter, but it was a nameless Eastern brand and stank abominably. Even stealing a bar of Air Mecca soap didn't help. At this point he became aware of a distant rumble and a RETURN TO YOUR SEAT light came on.

They were taking off.

He burst out of the door to discover that the skyjackers were oblivious to the lighted admonitions to FASTEN SEAT BELTS and NO SMOKING. They strolled about, clutching seat backs for support and smoking large cigars. It was a festive occasion for them. Tony, ever the law abider, slid into an empty seat and fastened his belt after carefully bringing his seat to an upright position. When he had finished this simple routine he looked down and saw the unconscious stewardess on the deck near his feet.

Dimly behind him great engines roared and acceleration pushed him deep into his seat. The girl on the floor did not move and she seemed safe enough there for the moment as they took off. If she were still alive. Skyjacking, kidnap and possibly murder—what fine people they were. As soon as the ship had leveled a bit Tony took off his safety belt and bent to touch the girl's forehead. It was warm enough and a pulse there throbbed nicely. Unconscious but not dead, with an ugly welt that vanished back under her hairline. There were four seats across here in the center section, and with the arms lifted up they made a comfortable couch. With some effort he picked the girl up and put her on the seats. While he was wondering what to do next her eyes opened and she looked at him blankly.

"Please," he said. "Don't shout or anything. All the other stewardesses are out of the plane—they must have missed you with all the excitement. We're airborne now."

"Who are you? Where are we going?" Quieter now, her English was almost perfect, with only a slight accent.

"Tony Hawkin, FBI. I brought the money aboard and have been skyjacked as well. And I have no idea where we are going."

"Praise Allah the others are safe, though I am of course sorry for you, Mr. Hawkin."

"Tony."

"Tony. I am Jasmin Sotiraki and I am senior in charge . . ."

"*¡Mira eso!*" "*¿Que tenemos aqui?*" "*¡Oye, Ramon!*"

The skyjackers were stirring about. The one called Jorge was standing in the aisle, gaping, calling out to one Ramon, who, it appeared, was their leader. He appeared, like a bad omen, almost instantly. He glared down at Jasmin, who sat up in the seat and exchanged glare for glare. The scratches on his face had been painted with Merthiolate and had clotted nicely. He was very angry.

"*Dile a esta puta que si causa una molestia o si habre la boca, la mataré. Dile.*"

"Look, Jasmin, this man is very angry. And he has absolute control. He says he will kill you if you do anything, even say anything, and I assure you he means it. Please."

"I will be all right," she said. Never taking her eyes away from the other's. He grunted—then reached out and slapped her wickedly. Her head rocked with the blow and inadvertent tears sprang to her eyes. But she said nothing, biting her lip, the red print of his hand clear on her skin. Ramon grunted again, then turned and went away.

"I will kill him," she whispered in Tony's ear. "One day I will kill him, but I will make no trouble now."

"That's nice," he said, and resisted the temptation to pat her hand, feeling, with some justification, that she was not the kind of girl who would like her hand patted at the moment. "Would you like a drink of water?"

"No thank you, I am fine."

"Perhaps a drink from the bar?" Hopefully.

"There is no bar. This is a Moslem airplane on the way to Mecca, there is no profanity of alcoholic beverage aboard other than that possessed by these *canaille*." So much for hope of profane beverage. He sighed inwardly.

"They seem to be well enough stocked with the stuff—as well as weapons. How did they get all this hardware aboard?"

"I am sure I have no idea. Look, there is the copilot out from the flight deck. Attend him quickly, he may know our destination."

Tony attended him as quickly as he could without drawing unwelcome attention from the gunmen and managed to intercept Tubby as he opened the rest room door.

"What's happened? Where are we going?"

"You don't mind, do you? It's been a long time between trips."

"Can't it wait a moment more?"

The copilot sighed. "Yes, I suppose it has to. We're off and on the way to Brussels, Belgium, if that is any help to you. And now, if you don't mind." The door closed with a positive click.

"Brussels?" Jasmin said. *"Mon Dieu—why there?* The Belge will arrest them instantly. I thought perhaps South America, where dictators can be bribed. Or Africa, anything can happen in Africa."

"It might well be Africa, and Brussels just a refueling stop."

"Callate y traenos comida. La muchacha te enseñara donde está."

It was Jorge, gun waving and obnoxious and more than a little drunk. Tony smiled falsely and nodded agreement.

"Come on, they want some food. We had better do just as they ask."

"I agree. It will also be an opportunity to bring food to the flight deck. They have had nothing all day."

She led Tony to the galley service center amidship where she opened the door of a tiny elevator. It was a snug fit for two, which he rather enjoyed and she appeared completely indifferent to. The galley was on the deck below, very complete with ovens, freezer and refrigerator compartments. Jasmin made herself very busy opening doors, turning on switches and sliding foil-covered platters into place. Tony examined gloomily the choice of drinks and decided against rose water and for orange juice. He poured a large glass, wished briefly for a double shot of vodka, then downed it and went to help Jasmin.

"Can I give you a hand?"

"It is not needed now, but later you may help bring the cart up."

There were cardboard containers on the meals, which she discarded as she loaded the food into the oven. The interesting six-sided star printed on the outside of them drew Tony's attention. He picked one out of the bag.

"Pride-of-Zion Kosher Chicken . . ."

"Throw that out," she snapped, tearing it from his hand and discarding it.

"Sorry but I thought, Arabs, you know . . ."

"I know indeed since I am Egyptian. But I am French educated and not as narrow of mind as some. Moslem and Jewish dietetic laws are similar indeed and these . . . meals you saw . . . are easily available from airport food suppliers. I am in charge of this, it is a small compromise. So if you would . . ."

Dark eyes rolled up toward him pleadingly, she could almost be an Apache girl with that skin and those eyes, and he melted instantly.

"Your secret is safe, I will never tell, never."

"You are very nice."

This time he did not resist the impulse to pat her hand and when he did so she smiled—then stood on tiptoe to kiss his cheek. Blood pounded nicely in his head and he reached for that delicate waist—here in the galley at 25,000 feet?—and his hands closed on air as she turned back to the oven.

After this came the thoroughly uninteresting task of getting carts in and out of the elevator and serving the bleary Cubans, while ignoring all the laughing offers of an apron and the shouts of *maricon, joto* and *pargo,* until he was finally permitted to serve the flight crew. It was dark on the flight deck, the cold stars outside appearing brighter than the hooded illumination of the instruments. The guard made them turn on the cabin lights, then watched closely as Tony served the food.

"Jasmin's aboard," he said. "She was knocked out by the head thug and shanghaied inadvertently."

"No more bad news, Hawkin," Captain Haycroft said thickly through a mouthful of stuffed derma. "They ordered clear airspace on all sides and I suppose we have it—though I think there are a couple of Air Force jets riding hard on us."

"Where are we?"

"Just clearing the tip of Newfoundland. Have a one hundred-knot tail wind, making good time. Routed over Ireland and England and right into Brussels. And no idea of what they will do then."

"*Basta de tanto hablar. Salte de aquí.*"

"Ugly here says I have to leave. Good luck."

"Thanks." Haycroft sawed patiently and unsuccessfully at the kosher chicken. "Try and cheer Jasmin up. Tell her we're sorry she's in this mess too."

Stunned by fatigue, food and drink, most of the skyjackers were asleep. When the trays had been cleaned away Tony felt a great urge to go to sleep too. It had been one of those kind of days and, streaking east like this, the sun would be up any minute now. Jasmin curled up by a window and he sat in the end of the same row, for whatever protection his presence could afford, and fell quickly into a restless slumber. This continued on and off for some time until right on schedule by mid-Atlantic time, 2 A.M. District of Columbia time, dawn sizzled in through the uncurtained windows. After this sleep was almost impossible and Tony went into and out of unconsciousness like a shutter going up and down. He had some strange dreams during these brief periods and one of them was about someone shaking him painfully by the shoulder and telling him to wake up, which dream, unhappily, proved to be true.

"Come on, sleeping beauty, stir yourself. You have work to do."

It was Ramon, the man in charge, now singularly the worse for wear. Gray stubble covered his jaws and his eyes were a sultry shade of red while his breath, a compound of kosher delicacies and strong rum, would have wilted a flower at twenty paces. Tony scrabbled awake and scrambled to his feet.

"What? What?" was the best his fatigue- and sleep-clotted mind could produce.

"These he-goat Englishmen in ground control say that they have no one who can speak Spanish. You must talk in English to them." In both colorful and profane language he said what he thought of the English as he pushed Tony toward the flight deck. In addition to the crew a number of interested Cubans had crowded in to join the fun and one of them, with microphone and earphones, was cursing into the radio an echo of their commander's complaints. He reluctantly surrendered the apparatus to Tony, who caught the end of the pained reply.

"*No hablar* Spanish here, do you understand, *ninguno*, oh bugger it, how does one say 'I don't understand'?"

"*¡Dile que se calle!*" Ramon snarled, poking his gun into Tony's side and holding one of the earphones to his own ear. Tony cleared his throat and pressed the press-to-talk button on the mike.

"I have been instructed to tell you to shut up."

"Sir! They have someone talking English on the skyjacked plane!"

There now followed much bilingual conversation and argument, with Tony in the middle, taking it from both sides until, at one moment, he found himself shouting Spanish into the microphone and talking to Ramon in English. A snarl and a gun prod terminated that rather quickly. Ramon appeared to understand some English, even if he did not speak it, and he issued his orders.

There were military planes following them, Ramon was sure of it, he could see their vapor trails. They must be sent away or he would throw out one or more of his hostages. With this in mind he ordered the DC-10 to a lower altitude so one of the doors could be opened. There were cries of anguish from ground control along with the assurance that there were no other aircraft anywhere in the vicinity. Despite this the plane dropped through a thick layer of cloud and the green British countryside could be seen through occasional gaps.

Clearance was guaranteed across southern England, the English Channel and on into Brussels. All flights had been stopped there and they were cleared for immediate landing.

As soon as these guarantees had been repeated a number of times Ramon cackled with laughter and tore the microphone and headphone wires out by their copper roots. He then, still laughing insanely, used his gun butt to pound the radio into scrap.

The RAF Vampire jets, high above and unseen by anyone

on the plane, lost visual contact with the DC-10 when it dropped below the cloud level. Ground radar also lost contact when the bulk of the Cotswold Hills interfered with their signals. But there were clear skies over the Channel so the chase planes rendezvoused there and waited for their quarry to emerge from the clouds. Coastal Command radar in Kent, Essex and Suffolk were also alerted and swung their great dishes around, eagerly awaiting the first tiny blip.

They waited. Then they waited some more and began to grow uneasy. Someone did some quick and simple math and discovered that the big plane was already twenty minutes late. By the time a half an hour had passed without its appearance a great amount of excited communication was taking place.

At the end of an hour it was admitted, albeit reluctantly, that the DC-10's whereabouts was completely unknown.

For all apparent purposes the great aircraft had completely vanished.

FOUR

"Hawkin," Captain Haycroft said in a very quiet voice, "I think he has flipped. Talk to him quietly, see if you can get him off the flight deck."

"Not flipped, just very happy as you can see," Ramon said cheerfully, rising from the ruin of the radio and spinning his pistol about his finger in Hollywood Western style.

"You speak English?" Tony said, memories of the last shouted simultaneous translation session still tingling in his ears.

"How *bright* of you to notice, Señor FBI Man."

There was a muffled curse from the large skyjacker who stood in the flight-deck entrance. He was attempting to pull his burnoose off over his head and had become entangled in the folds. Another Cuban went to his aid and freed him and helped him to remove the encumbering garment. When it was off he appeared far less Cuban than he had earlier—in fact he did not look Cuban at all. His face and hands had been stained brown, but his bare arms were pale, freckled and hairy, while his clothing was even more interesting. There were shoulder tabs and brass buttons on his military-type khaki shirt. He wore open sandals, knee-length socks—and a kilt with pendant sporran before. Ramon cackled with joy at this sight and slapped his leg with pleasure.

"We have done it, Angus, have we not?"

"Aye, so far. Now move out so we can see that it ends right."

The automatic pilot flew the great plane easily and alone, for all of the flight crew had their bulging eyes on the transformed skyjacker. Events were running far ahead of comprehension. First an English-speaking Cuban who spoke only Spanish. Now a nontalking Cuban who was really a Scot. Angus fractured the moment by shouldering Tony roughly aside and stalking forward to loom over the captain. He produced a map from his sporran and shoved it under Haycroft's nose.

"Point out where we are," he ordered.

In silence, Haycroft consulted his course and the bearings on his own map that showed radio fixes, then compared both maps until he touched a spot lightly with his index finger.

"We're just about here."

"You'll no be lying to me?" There was unconcealed violence in Angus's voice and, to emphasize the question, he pulled a gleaming dirk from a sheath in his stocking and held it lightly to the captain's throat.

Haycroft was calm, ignoring both threat and knife, his voice unemotional and quiet. "I do not know who you are—nor do I care. But I am captain of this aircraft and responsible for its safety and the safety of my passengers. I do not lie about these matters."

Angus only grunted noncommittally in answer and frowned over his map. "Now then. Take this kite down under the clouds and turn to a course of a hundred and twelve degrees and follow it for a wee bit."

"I cannot do that. The clouds are at five thousand and there are hills here and . . ."

This time the point of the dagger pressed hard into the flesh of his neck so that a bright drop of blood formed on the tip.

"Now then," Angus spoke in the quietest of whispers. "You will do as I say or I will drive this knife home and ask the co-pilot to fly the aircraft."

They locked their gazes tightly—and it was Haycroft who turned away first. He disengaged the automatic pilot and began a slow turn to starboard, losing altitude at the same time. Angus straightened up and took the knife from the pilot's neck—but kept it ready in his hand as he called back over his shoulder:

"Ramon—get everyone out of here except yourself."

Tony left with the other skyjackers on his heels and the door slammed behind him. Jasmin Sotiraki was awake and sitting up, her large eyes questioning as he went and sat beside her.

"You are not going to believe what I have to tell you."

"I believe anything of these *cochons*."

"Would you believe that the boss, Ramon, speaks perfect English and the entire Spanish-speaking thing is some kind of complex hoax?"

"What kind of hoax?"

"I have no idea—but that big skyjacker, the Cuban disguised as an Arab is really a Scotchman . . . don't look at me in that funny way. I'm telling you the truth. And the two things *have* to tie in together. The entire Spanish bit was so everyone should think about Cubans." He snapped his fingers and a gleam of newfound intelligence burned in his eye. "Think Cuban and *not* Scotch! But why? Because Scotland is hooked onto England and we are over England right now, flying low. Which could mean . . ."

The whir, grind and thunk from below their seats finished the sentence for him.

"The landing gear has been lowered," Jasmin said redundantly.

"We're coming in for a landing."

Tony jumped to the window and saw brilliant green fields and trees rushing by below, a stream, then a village, then they were lower still. He hammered on the seat with his fist.

"Brussels, the Spanish bit, everything was misdirection. This is where we were heading all the time."

The seat-belt light came on and, after some preliminary scratching, Haycroft's voice sounded through the plane.

"This is the captain speaking. We are coming in for a landing and I think it is going to be a very rough, perhaps disastrous landing. I will do my best but you must take all precautions possible. You must be seated. Sit well back in your seats and pull your seat belts tight. Then bend forward and take your ankles in your hands. This position is the best protection possible. I repeat . . ."

He did not repeat. The microphone must have been taken away from him because Ramon came on and, in a slightly shrill voice, repeated the captain's instructions in Spanish. There was an immense bustle as the skyjackers rushed to find seats. Tony did as he had been instructed after a last, horrified glance at the treetops streaming by, apparently just under the extended landing flaps on their wings. A strobe light in the wing tip was flashing cheerily.

Down they drifted and farther down. Tony steeled himself for the impact, which seemed endlessly delayed. Jasmin, also bent over and clutching her ankles, smiled at him warmly: the stewardess doing her job to the end. What end? His heart began to thud like a triphammer as though getting the most out of its last moments.

A giant impact shook the fabric of the airplane, which instantly began to vibrate and shake as though the wheels were running over railroad ties. At the same time the power was reversed in the engines and 120,000 pounds of thrust fought to stop the hurtling weight. The terrible hammering continued—they were suddenly hurled sideways and Jasmin screamed—then they were going straight again.

Until, with a last groaning bounce, heave and skew, the ship settled forward, shuddered and stopped. The engines whined down into silence.

They were on the ground.

With shaking fingers Tony snapped open his belt and sat up. In the last seconds of its spectacular landing the DC-10 had stopped running straight so, when it had finally halted, it was standing crossways on the runway. Through the window Tony could see about two hundred feet of dusty, narrow concrete with weeds growing up through the cracks in the slabs. Beyond the end of the runway was green grass, a fence and the hind ends of a number of cows who were departing in some haste across the meadow. He knew just how they felt. He turned to Jasmin, who was sitting up, looking very pale and fanning herself with a magazine.

"Are you all right?"

She nodded weakly. "Yes. But I must just sit quiet for a few moments."

She was the only quiet one. The instant the plane had stopped the flight-deck door had burst open and, at gunpoint, the flight crew had been rudely thrust out. Captain Haycroft came last, propelled along swiftly by the burly Scot. Battery power was still on, for the lights burned cheerfully and the door opened smoothly when the handle was pulled. Since he was being ignored for the moment, Tony slipped to the rear of the plane, as unobtrusively as he could, and looked out of a window on the port side.

He discovered what all the bumping had been about. Stretching off into the distance was the runway, terminating in a group of seedy and dilapidated buildings: a deserted airport obviously, built for aircraft of a different age. Smaller aircraft undoubtedly, because when the ponderous DC-10 had landed it had dropped right through the concrete of the runway and had plowed up the entire length of it. Three deep ruts, twisting and turning from time to time, led right up to the airplane, dark soil mixed with broken chunks of concrete. And there, racing along beside the runway in a boiling cloud of dust, were a car, a truck and a bright red fire engine. His appreciation of this fascinating sight was interrupted by a now familiar jab of a gun muzzle into his tender ribs accompanied by an order to go forward with the others.

The two pilots, the flight engineer and Jasmin had been herded into the front rows of seats across the plane from the open door. Tony joined them there under the shepherding muzzle of a submachine gun. They all watched the events in progress with a great deal of interest; this included the guard, who kept looking over his shoulder. There was a good deal of shouting outside and moments later the top of a ladder, rising like an elevator, appeared at the door with its rider, a solid-looking man who could have been a close relative of Angus—who instantly spoke to the newcomer in a far from brotherly way.

"Are you daft bringing that bloody great fire engine? It'll be reported and the police will be right behind you."

"We had to, laddie. Painter's van with the ladders broke down —this was all we could steal in time. You have it, the money?"

Memory of this cheered Angus, who smiled for the first time.

"Och, aye! Two million of those American bank notes. Let's be off."

As though these words were a summoning cue there could be heard a distant clanging of alarm bells rapidly growing louder. "The rozzers!" the man on the ladder cried, and instantly vanished from sight.

Everyone stared. Clearly framed in the open doorway was a now familiar cloud of dust and racing vehicle. Only this car was a low black sedan topped with flashing lights and loud with jangling alarm bell.

At last the gun-waving Cubans had something to bang away at and they made the most of the opportunity. With an ear-splitting roar of sound every machine gun and pistol went off, while one enthusiast even hurled a hand grenade that exploded far closer to the plane than the approaching vehicle, sending fragments whining and thudding into the DC-10's skin. Spurts of dust rose up all around the police car, most far wide of the mark as the guns jumped about in unaccustomed hands. But a message of sorts was received by the policemen, for the car swerved wildly, spun about and drove behind the high dirt walls of a bunker where it vanished from sight. Clouds of dust rose from the walls of this revetment but, since it had obviously been built to shield an airplane from heavy bomb fragments, the screaming bullets had no effect. After a great deal of shouting and pushing Ramon managed to stop the firing. In the resultant silence an amplified voice could clearly be heard.

"This is the police. You are involved in the commission of a serious crime and have fired upon us. You will surrender at once."

The only response to this were some colorful Gaelic and Spanish oaths and a few more shots.

"Quickly. Out of the plane before they return the fire," Ramon shouted. Angus looked at him with scorn.

"The police have no guns. But they do have radios, which is worse. Let's unload. We have the two vehicles and we'll rendezvous as planned . . ."

"We must have hostages to prevent capture."

"It's no wise."

"It's the wisest thing we can do. We'll take the girl and the FBI man, one in each car. The police won't dare stop us."

The big Scot started to protest, then shrugged. "All right—but let's go *now!*"

"*Everyone out!*" Ramon ordered and there was a dive and struggle in the entrance. Before leaving he snapped open the suitcase and took out a bundle of hundred dollar bills and threw it to Jorge with a sharp order. Angus scowled at this, but said nothing. Jasmin screamed in ineffectual protest as she and Tony were bundled swiftly down the ladder. The last he saw of her was when she was being pushed into the back of the high, thin truck labeled ACME STEAM LAUNDRY along with most of the Cubans. The newly arrived Scot jumped behind the wheel of an elegant maroon Rolls-Royce. Angus pushed Tony into the front seat next to him, then climbed in himself. Ramon was wedged in the center of the back seat with one of his Cuban gunmen on each side of him. The suitcase with the money was on his lap, clutched tightly. The instant they were all in place the engine hummed to life and the car surged smoothly down the runway and away, while the truck vanished in the opposite direction.

"The truck is slow," Ramon said, looking back out of the rear window. "It can be followed, seen, stopped . . ."

"Not to worry," Angus reassured him. "They only have eight miles to go, it's all been worked out. There is a bit of forest there with a narrow track. The van will block it, it's stolen in any case, while they get away in the other cars. A half mile after that and they will be on the M2 motorway and well on their way. We'll be doing the same thing a bit further on."

The skyjackers seemed reassured by this, but Tony wished they wouldn't talk so graphically. He knew perfectly well what happened to hostages who knew too much. Sinking lower in the seat he tried to think himself invisible. With effortless ease the big car slid silently along the narrow track between the hedges, then twisted around a corner to an even narrower road that ran beside a high stone wall. A right-angle turn brought them into a lane covered by arching trees and revealed a farm tractor sideways across the road before them.

Tony had a split second to brace himself against the dash as the brakes locked and they screeched to a shuddering halt with the bumper lightly touching the high tractor wheel.

On the instant both Scots turned and dived into the rear seat. By accident or design they both also used Tony's shoulders as launching pads. Large hands grabbed and pushed hard and he was forced down and out of the seat. A thrashing boot caught him in the back of the head, steel hobnails biting deep, and he ended up twisted and feeling half broken, dazed and gasping, jammed under the dash with his legs splayed out on the seat above him.

As in a nightmare he saw great ugly men loom up on all sides of the car, staring through the windows, tearing open the doors in back. They were wielding bicycle chains like heavy whips, effectively too if the thuds and screams meant anything.

It was over in a matter of seconds. The men vanished, there was the quick sound of running feet and an automobile engine that raced wildly. Gears were engaged with a jangling clash and the sound of the car dimmed and vanished.

With infinite care Tony writhed around onto the front seat then, clutching the back, rose up slowly. Other than the tractor the road was empty. Birds sang sweetly among the branches above. Two of the skyjackers were sprawled motionlessly, half in and half out of the car, blood oozing slowly from their battered heads. Ramon sat, unmoving, in the middle of the rear seat staring at Tony.

"Don't blame me, it wasn't my idea."

The Cuban did not answer. Then Tony noticed that his tongue hung limply from between his teeth and that his head lay at a most unnatural angle. Tony reached out and waved his hand inches away from the staring eyes; they did not move.

Even before he looked around Tony knew that the suitcase of money would not be there.

FIVE

It had been quickly and efficiently done. The roadblock, the sudden attack—all that Angus and the driver had to do was see that the Cubans did not draw their weapons for a few seconds until the reinforcements arrived. Brutal and sure. Tony opened the door and climbed shakily out. The birds still sang with great enthusiasm and from behind the hedges in the nearby field there came a sudden crashing like a large animal about to attack. Tony, still groggy, pulled a limp skyjacker farther out into the road and patted his clothes; he had a gun in his jacket pocket. It came free with some struggle, a short-nosed revolver of some kind, and Tony turned and faced the source of the thrashing. Were they coming back to finish him off? He would sell his life dearly. His thoughts were still fuzzy and when he shook his head to clear it it only hurt more.

What was he worried about? If they had wanted to kill him they could have done that before they left. Hesitantly, he strode over to the hedge, gun ready, and looked behind it.

A man lay there, trussed in ropes, with a red bandanna handkerchief stuffed into his mouth and tied in place. He wore high rubber boots, dirt-splattered trousers, was gray of hair and red of skin—and bulging his eyes at Tony so they stood out of his head.

"Oh, sorry." Tony put the gun away. "I thought they were coming back." He ungagged the man and bent to untie his ropes.

"Ptah! Dirty buggers. Asked me the way they did then, bash, and me off the tractor and in the weeds. I'll have the law . . ."

"Just the thing. Look, there is more involved in this than you realize. I'll stay here and make sure these hijackers don't leave—"

"Hijackers, aye! Hijacked my tractor."

"They've done more than that. Look, get to a phone or the police. Tell them we have some of the airplane skyjackers here. Can you do that?"

"Aye."

The farmer shook off the coils of rope, looked with some interest at the sprawled bodies, then started the tractor and trundled off down the road. Tony left Ramon sightlessly staring in the car, but dragged, not too gently, the other two to the side of the road. They were beginning to stir and moan as he tied their hands behind their backs with pieces of the discarded rope.

Within a few moments both skyjackers came to, moaning and complaining, shaking their bonds helplessly. They cursed at each other and at Castro, Scotland and life in particular while Tony nodded in appreciation of their vocabulary. Only when they started on him did he shake the gun in their direction so they cowered back, then he repeated with some warmth all the insults they had lavished on him during his captivity. It gave him a great deal of pleasure and did no harm so he was feeling much better by the time the police arrived.

Aroused by telephone, the local constable was the first to appear. He came down the lane on a large black bicycle, pedaling easily. After leaning the bicycle carefully against the hedge he took out a leather-covered note pad and a stub of pencil, carefully licking the pencil tip before he spoke.

"That is a gun you have in your possession, isn't it, sir?"

"I hope so since I am holding prisoner two men who are wanted for international skyjacking of a very expensive airplane, plus extortion of the sum of two million dollars."

"Are they indeed!" The policeman nodded appreciatively and sternly. "Would you give me the gun, sir? Possession of a weapon is a crime with which I do not think you wish to be charged." He stepped close and held out his hand. Tony passed it over.

"Quite right, Officer, since they are your prisoners now."

"Indeed they are, sir." He looked closely at the weapon, found the safety and flicked it in into place, then, before Tony's horrified gaze, put it into his pocket.

"I wouldn't do that . . ."

"That's all right, sir, I wouldn't worry if I were you. Now if I could have a statement. Time nine twenty-five, A.M." He entered this slowly and one of the skyjackers jumped to his feet and ran down the road.

With an easy motion the constable threw his nightstick so it went between the Cuban's legs, sending him sprawling. Before he could rise he was seized by the collar, pulled to his feet, marched back and dropped beside his companion. They both followed the loose-swinging club with their eyes and drew back.

"Now you lot don't want to cause any trouble, do you?"

"They don't speak English, Officer."

"No matter, sir, there are other forms of communication." The nightstick spoke this language sharply as he smacked it into his palm. Bells rang cheerily down the road and a moment later a police car with four occupants braked to a stop. The constable saluted as they poured out.

"Would anyone like to hear what happened?" Tony said brightly as they turned to face him. "Not a half an hour ago a man was killed here and two million dollars carried away. I can attempt to describe the men who did it—if you are interested?"

They were, and he did, and with much hurried work on the radio the forces of law and order spread wide their search. Tony noticed that one of the policemen stayed very close to him for quite some time, until confirmation came in that he really was a kidnapped FBI man, not one of the skyjackers. With this information also came the order to get him to London as soon as possible. For this purpose a police car puttered up and was put at his disposal, something smaller and a good deal humbler than the car the sergeant had arrived in—a label on the hood said it was a Morris Minor—as well as a plainclothes detective named Finch. After a few miles Tony wished that a Morris Major had been provided, if there were a car by that name, as well as a driver who could say more than "ngh." Finch, for all of his undoubted sterling worth as a law enforcement officer, could not have talked less if he had had lockjaw. He bent forward firmly, tiny steering wheel clutched in brawny hands, brows beetling fiercely in concentration, and put all of his attention to the driving. After a few attempts at conversation Tony slumped, surly and uncomfortable, in his seat, looked out at the landscape—and began to cheer up.

He was in England! The reality finally slipped through. His first time here. An inadvertent trip, indeed, but at least the price was right. For him; the two million bucks was someone else's concern. He had braved danger and skyjackers, kept his cool in tight situations and apprehended two of the crooks. Not bad for a small-town Indian art major turned FBI man. All of this would look good in his civil service record. Another promotion might even be in order. And, since he was here against his will, they would have to transport him home as well. Perhaps he ought to stay and help with the investigation, that was a good idea, get in a little sightseeing at the same time. Mother of Parliaments, Runnymede, Stratford-on-Avon! There would be plenty to see and do. His numbed posterior was forgotten in the pleasures of anticipation.

The countryside, which until this moment had been completely pastoral, cows, copses, farmhouses, fields of grain, brooks and such, now changed abruptly as they swung with trepidation onto a sort of parkway. It was a miniaturized version of the Jersey Turnpike, which it greatly resembled, despite the fact that the cars were driving on the wrong side of the road. This seemed to work all right as long as all of the drivers were aware of the reversal. The police car hurled itself along at a dramatic thirty miles an hour through the landscape, which was about the same landscape you might see along any highway in the Western World. There were tantalizing glimpses of Olde England from time to time, but not many. Coming around a turn they had a good view, for a number of seconds, of a white stone building with a thatch roof, over the door of which hung a colorful sign-board that read GRAVEDIGGERS ARMS. Memory of many British films struck him quickly and he groped around for the word, pointing a fluttering finger.

"That building, there, the white one with the sign. Is that, what do you call it, a *pub?*"

Finch flicked a quick official eye in the direction of the build-ing and after a ruminative moment produced a reluctant "aye." Tony watched earnestly as it faded from sight.

"They have drinks there, don't they? Food too?"

After much thought, words failing him apparently, Finch nod-ded his head.

"That's really great. Listen, would you stop at the next one, I haven't eaten since yesterday sometime and could really use a drink too."

"No pubs on motorway."

"Well then pull off the motorway," Tony said peevishly. "A few minutes won't make any difference to Scotland Yard but will make a big difference with me."

Finch rolled the thought around for quite a while, looking at all sides of it with careful police scrutiny, yet could find no fault. The result was a final muttered "aye" as he turned off at the next exit. A few hundred yards down the road was a half-timbered establishment called The Royal Oak. It looked like he was in luck, royal! Here was a place where perhaps the king came to drink, or was it a queen now? They parked and entered a door labeled SALOON BAR, which certainly sounded like a step in the right direction.

The interior was all he had imagined and then some. Hum of low voices, rattle of glasses, bottles and glassware twinkling in the mirror behind the bar.

"Yes, gentlemen, may I help you?" said a round, red, pleasant woman who stood framed by her wares.

"I'm for that," Tony said. "What do you recommend, Mr. Finch?"

"Pint of bitter," Finch said darkly. It didn't sound too optimistic but Tony went along and had one himself. The bar woman pumped industriously on a large black handle and filled two glass tubs with an amber liquid which, while being flatter and a bit warmer than the beer he knew, certainly was better in every other way.

"That will be thirty pence, if you please."

"I'll get this," Tony said, easily beating the policeman to the wallet draw. He pushed a five dollar bill across the dark wood and the woman looked at it dubiously.

"Only real money here, sir, I don't know what that is."

Abraham Lincoln scowled up blackly from the bill, having been reduced by an air flight to a specie of Monopoly paper. Finch nodded somberly, as though he had expected no better, and placed a many-sided silver coin on the bar.

"Look, I'm sorry about that. If you'll pay for the drinks and lunch I'll pay you back, really I will." Finch nodded again in obvious disbelief.

Mention of lunch stirred a gastric rumble of expectancy and an inquiry regarding food led him to the glass cabinet at the end of the same bar. Here, as though in a museum, a number of unfamiliar objects were on display. He did recognize the baked beans, but they were obviously cold and he did not even like them when hot. There was a plate bearing a number of fuzzy brown spheres resembling tinted tennis balls and he pointed them out to the bar woman, who hovered close with plate and knife.

"I'll have one of those. What are they?"

"Scotch eggs, sir. Bit of pickle with that?"

"Of course, whatever you say." The object rested heavily on the plate set before him and he still had no idea what it was. He pressed on it with the knife and it skidded sideways without being dented. Finally, by holding it steady with his fingers, he managed to bisect it. A hard-boiled egg was revealed in the center surrounded by chopped meat of some kind. It was, however, quite delicious and he finished it quickly along with the tart relish and managed to down a second one with no difficulty.

Finch drained his glass and looked pointedly at his watch. Tony very quickly gathered in the last crumb, emptied his glass and hurried out to the car.

After this the trip was most uneventful and Tony dozed, jumped on by the fatigue of the past hours. He awoke briefly when the motorway dumped them into city traffic, but this did not disturb him long. Mexico City traffic was more insane, Washington, D.C., more crowded. The only difference here was the fact the cars were all smaller so more could be crowded in. Which didn't make much difference since the streets were narrower too. He slept and awoke only when they pulled to a halt in a street that, appropriately, was labeled GREAT SCOTLAND YARD. With little ceremony he was ushered into the tiny, old-fashioned office of Inspector Smivey. The inspector, a thin jack-knife of a man, with a fringe of gray hair surrounding a polished bald head, tufts of the same hair sprouting elegantly from his ears and nostrils, rose long enough to shake his hand quickly, wave him to a chair, then sink back into his own again.

"I'm afraid you have been through a rather trying experience, Mr. Hawkin."

"It could have been much worse. Has anything been found out about the stewardess, Jasmin Sotiraki? She wasn't in the truck when they found it, I was told."

"I know you will be happy to hear that she was found, unhurt, not ten minutes ago. Here in London, in the suburbs. Now— would you mind terribly if I took a statement from you and had someone in to transcribe it?"

"No, of course not."

The inspector muttered into an intercom. Over his shoulder, through the window, a square tower with a peaky top was clearly seen. It had a very large clock set into it which, at that moment, began to ring the hour of three. It sounded very familiar, like the recordings of Big Ben he had heard. Could it possibly be . . . ?

"Now, Mr. Hawkin, if you could start with the moment you first boarded the plane in Washington."

It was a simple enough tale, still frighteningly clear in memory, and he told it in a rush, the secretary's pencil skimming across the paper. When he was done, Inspector Smivey took him over the story again with some specific questions.

"You stated that one bundle of hundred dollar notes was taken away in the truck by one of the Cubans, Jorge, while Angus and his associates appear now to have the rest?"

"That's right."

"Now what were these instructions you overheard when the leader, Ramon, gave the money to this Jorge?"

"He said something about taking these to show to the something-or-other. I couldn't quite make out the last word. It sounded like *emcubrilor* or *encubridor*."

"Would you write the word down here just as you heard it?"

Tony did and the paper was taken away. At the same time Jasmin was ushered in through the still open door.

"Tony! Then you are not dead. I was so worried." She embraced him briefly, but before he could return the embrace she pulled away and sat down.

"I was more worried about you, it's been hours since they took you away."

"There is not the need to tell me! *Cochons!* From one car to another, the blindfold, riding and riding until, zip, I am in the street with runners in my best pantyhose. So I call 999 and am here."

"Nine, nine, nine?"

"The emergency number anywhere in the British Isles," Inspector Smivey patiently explained. "You might remember it for future reference. Now, if you would be so kind as to wait in the outer office one of my people will get back to you. We have contacted the American authorities about an emergency passport. In the meantime we are arranging for a room for you in a hotel nearby and would appreciate it if you were to go there and remain until we contact you."

"I'm for that. It's been a long day—or days."

Jasmin waved weakly when he left and in the outer office he

found the copilot, Tubby Waterbury, sprawled on a sofa and reading a newspaper. A black headline read "SKYJACK MURDER VICTIM LOOTED."

"Glad to see you got out of this in one piece, Hawkin."

"I feel the same way. How's the plane?"

"Going no place fast. Haycroft refused to leave it except at gunpoint so I came down to brief them. That airport, Tilbury Hill, used to be a bomber base in the Second World War. No one's been near it since. That damned runway is no harder than baked mud."

The inspector poked his head out of the door. "Mr. Hawkin. Could that word have been *encubridor?*"

"Sounds right. But I never heard it before."

"It apparently means a fence, receiver of stolen goods, in Cuban slang. That would make sense in context, would it not?"

"Positively. They needed the money as a sample for the fence to see. If that's what the word means."

"It does. Our Spanish Department is quite knowledgeable. A messenger will be here for you in a moment. A room's been booked at the Regent Palace Hotel, which, so I'm given to understand, is favored by your countrymen."

"Tourists," Tubby said as soon as the inspector had vanished. "Full of them. Right on Piccadilly Circus. Traffic will keep you awake all night."

"Mr. Hawkin?" a young, pert, long-haired and short-skirted girl in a tight sweater asked, smiling. "I'm to take you to the hotel." He nodded like a simpleton and followed obediently, wondering at all the stories he had heard about the undersexed and ugly English girls.

The cab ride was all too brief and she unhappily departed as soon as he was given his room key. The bellhop widened his eyes a bit at the lack of luggage, but they shrank back to normal when he was presented with an American dollar bill, which, he assured Tony, he would have no trouble cashing even though it was devalued. The room was on the smallish side and furnished in early British nothing, while the roar of traffic did come in clearly through the window. However, after a search he found a phone, a number for room service and a menu. He settled for a sandwich and some beer after a linguistic struggle with a strangely accented person at the other end of the line. Then he stripped off his shirt and picked at the tape that held the gigli saw in place about his wrist. It would not come free easily so he decided to ignore it and washed the dust of England from it as well as his arm and the rest of his easily accessible skin. His chin was decidedly scratchy; after he ate he would have to think about getting a shave and, if possible, a clean shirt. Cash in what little money he had, then find the American Embassy and get some more. Nineteen dollars was not going to take him very far.

He was scrubbing himself dry with the towel when the subservient knock sounded on the door. So quickly! There was much to be said for the service here, fastest he had ever experienced.

When he threw the door open a small dark man wearing sunglasses and a fuzzy beard moved swiftly in and closed the door behind him.

"The money, where eez eet?" he said and, as though for punctuation, balled his brown leather-gloved fist and buried it deep in Tony's midriff.

SIX

It was a nasty blow that sent Tony staggering back across the room, doubled over with pain. Since the bed was only a few feet from the door it struck him behind the knees and he collapsed backward onto it.

"Speek," the intruder said, stalking menacingly after Tony with hard fist raised, easily dodging a feeble kick.

"Listen. What are you talking about? I have no money. A few dollars in my wallet. You can have it."

"Two meelion dollars."

"*That* money. You should have said so. The last I saw of it it was vanishing with a tall Scotchman named Angus and a number of his friends."

"Where they go?"

"I have no idea . . . *ouch!*"

The fist struck again and, impelled by the pain, Tony rolled off the far side of the bed. His assailant came around the end and Tony picked up the chair. At the same instant there was a light tapping on the door. The bearded man extracted a gun from his pocket and pointed it at Tony. "Who eez eet?"

"Room service. I ordered some food." The gun vanished, though its outline was clear in the other's pocket. "Answer eet. A wrong move and *pan* you are dead."

"Don't worry, don't worry." Tony padded to the door and opened it to reveal a slim, dark woman with a sheaf of papers in her hand. Tony crossed his hands over his bare chest and gaped.

"Mr. Hawkin? I'm the assistant manager. I'm sorry to disturb you but there is some question about the registration. If I could come in? Thank you."

She entered well before he could answer her, smiled at the scowling bearded man, then consulted her papers.

"It seems you have not entered your passport number, nor have you paid in advance for the room, which is our normal policy. You must realize . . ." Behind her back the gunman was making jerking motions toward the door with his head while grating his teeth. The message was unmistakable. Tony broke in.

"Look, miss, if you please. That was all explained when I was sent here by Scotland Yard."

"Really?" Her eyebrows climbed higher and higher. "Are there charges involved? I don't think the hotel approves of this."

"No, not that, the opposite. It was all explained."

"Well not to *me* I'm sorry to say. If you don't mind I'll just ring up the office."

Muttering darkly over her papers, she went to the phone and picked up the receiver. When she did this the gunman turned away from her toward Tony, rolling his eyes downward and showing the shape of the gun in his pocket.

As soon as his back was turned to her, the girl raised the telephone handpiece high—then brought it down sharply on the back of his neck. He slumped to the floor without a sound. Tony tried not to gape.

"Sorry about this, Mr. Hawkin. But when I saw him following you I thought there might be trouble. The hand on gun in pocket rather convinced me. He was up to no good I assume?"

"He hit me. But, you . . . he . . ."

"Him? He's an Al Fatah muscleman we have been watching. My name is Esther Ben-Alter. We had orders from an old friend of yours to keep an eye on you, render help if needed. When I saw this *kelev* going up to your room I thought I might look in."

Tony was struggling into his shirt and getting more confused every instant. "Old friend?"

"Jacob Goldstein. He sends his best wishes."

"Then you're an Israeli. Al Fatah, Palestinians . . ."

"You're catching on." She bent over the unconscious agent and relieved him of his gun. "We have been doing a little investigating into Air Mecca for a long time, since some of the financing behind it isn't too kosher. There's Palestinian resistance money in it and we think they have other plans besides pilgrim transportation. Which is our problem, not yours. Jacob says we are to help you in any way we can. Take this card, it's a bakery that is also our cover. There's someone there all the time. Say 'onion bagel' and you'll be connected to the right parties. Now, if you'll give me a hand with this one we'll get rid of him. Be careful when you open the door from now on. Apparently they don't look on the skyjacking of their own planes the same way they do others."

Fortunately the hall was empty, as was the automatic elevator when they rang for it. Esther held the door while Tony dragged the Al Fatah agent in and propped him up in the corner. The doors closed on him with a pneumatic sigh and he slid away.

"Please don't go yet," Tony asked. "I do have some questions and I need some help, like where can I get a razor? Things like that."

"My pleasure."

They were back in the room for no more than a few moments when there was a rapid knocking on the door. Tony shied away from it; there was just too much activity for him. "Who is it?" he called out. A muffled voice muttered something about room service.

"Answer it," Esther whispered, hand behind back, Arab gun ready in hand. He opened the door cautiously. A white-coated Indian, turban-wearing Indian, not his kind, stood patiently outside at the helm of a wheeled cart.

"My order? In here, thanks."

Saliva pumped at the sight of the many layers of crust-trimmed white bread, bits of turkey, bacon and tomato peeking shyly from the edge, brown bottled beer to one side.

"I'm not disturbing you, am I, Hawkin?" a familiar voice asked.

Inspector Smivey was in the hall, derby hat on head, tight-rolled umbrella in hand. He was talking to Tony but his eyes were fixed steadily on Esther. She returned the cold gaze with a warm smile and bent to retrieve the sheaf of blank paper from the floor where she had dropped it. She spoke before Tony could.

"How do you do, Inspector? I have been interviewing Mr. Hawkin for an article for my paper. We have a great interest in skyjackings where Arabs are involved, as you can well imagine?"

"But this was an *Arab* plane that was skyjacked, Miss Ben-Alter."

"Same cast of characters, Inspector. But I am sure you have important matters to talk over with Mr. Hawkin so I will be going. Thank you so much for your time, Mr. Hawkin. Good-bye."

She slipped out, still smiling, with the inspector's scowls following in her wake. The waiter rattled dishes and opened the beer bottle. "Extraordinary," the inspector said. "Drunks at this time of day. There was a foreign chap sleeping it off in the lift when I came up. Tourist I imagine."

The Indian waited, dark-eyed and patient in the doorway, and Tony gave him one of his diminishing stock of dollar bills, symbol of Indian-Indian compatibility, then closed the door behind him.

"I would watch out for that woman if I were you," the inspector said.

"Newswoman?" Tony said innocently around a large mouthful of sandwich.

"Yes. She wants you to think that. Some sort of Israeli agent. Up to no good I'm sure. In any case, hope you don't mind my dropping in." Mumble of understanding through mouthful of sandwich and beer. "I wanted to ask you if you would mind stopping by the Yard tonight to look at our identification files. Mug books I believe you call them. I won't be there but you'll be expected. Be of great help to us. Your skyjacker Angus turns out to be Angus Macpherson, one of the moving figures in the Free Scotland movement. We have been looking for him on a number of other charges, to which we have now added murder. He was a judo chap in the forces, that broken neck looks very much like his work. If you go through the pictures perhaps you can pick out some of his mates."

Tony belched lightly and sighed. "I'll be happy to go, Inspector."

"Five-minute walk. Just head down Regent Street right off the Circus here, down the steps and the Yard is just across from the New Admiralty Building there, the great ugly thing with all the masts on top that looks like a beached battleship. We've identified the dead man too, Ramon Garcia, Cuban in exile, troublemaker. Been in and out of your American jails for possession of weapons, things like that. The other two you captured are part of his group. Any questions?" The inspector tweaked lightly at one of the hairs sprouting from his ears.

"Have you heard anything about my passport?"

"Your embassy is sending a chap around here at ten tomorrow morning. He can take care of any other problems you might have."

Inspector Smivey let himself out and Tony locked the door carefully behind him. The gigli saw under his wrist itched and he scratched at it and thought of taking it off. But it wasn't the sort of thing you liked to leave lying around, unless you were a brain surgeon that is, and in the end he left it in place. He was tired and really did not feel like going out, but he had promised the inspector. Maybe the fresh air would wake him up. He yawned widely as he was tying his tie before the bathroom mirror, and saw that he was developing nice black splotches under his eyes. The life of an international operator is never an easy one. But . . . Scotland Yard needed him, and an agent is never off duty. Squaring his shoulders, he left the room—after first making a careful survey of the corridor.

Tourists of many nationalities crowded the lobby and he pushed through a babble of strange tongues and exotic dress to the street outside. It was dark now and Piccadilly Circus blazed with lights and boomed with traffic, spreading before his eyes the opening shot in almost every English motion picture ever made. A man with a cloth cap and the voice of a bullhorn was selling newspapers on the sidewalk and shouting something incomprehensible, but a large sheet posted next to him advertised "NEW SKYJACK REVELATIONS" in black letters. Tony wished he had some of the local coin to buy those revelations. Never mind, he could ask about them in the Yard. He strolled through the milling early evening crowds, admiring the signs and the shop windows, almost being killed when he stepped off the curb into whirring traffic and looked in the wrong direction.

There was less traffic when he came to Pall Mall, the first street he had ever seen that was named after a cigarette, but he stopped nevertheless while he figured out which way to look. Right, that was it, not left, and he looked right and saw only a large black car slowly approaching.

"Do you have a light for my cigarette?" a voice asked behind him and he was turning to say no before he realized that the voice had spoken in Spanish—not English. He turned faster and saw the familiar and unwelcome face of the skyjacker Jorge.

"You are under arrest," he said firmly, and wondered how he would go about implementing that. Jorge grinned widely, then planted his shoulder against Tony's chest and pushed.

The black car had stopped behind them with the rear door open. Tony shot into it nicely and strong hands pinioned him. As he struggled Jorge fell in on top of him, the door slammed and they were away. Tony stopped struggling at the now familiar sight of guns and sighed. His newfound popularity for armed villains was something he could just as well do without.

"You are prepared to co-operate with us?" the man behind him said, speaking what Tony was beginning to recognize all too clearly as Cuban Spanish. He turned about to face his questioner, a sturdy, dark-haired man of middle years, firm-jawed and hawk-nosed, wearing a black eye patch. Tony recognized him from newspaper pictures.

"The Cuban Moshe Dayan?"

"I prefer my own name, Colonel Jaime Juarez-Sedoño. The co-operation?"

"You're holding the gun, Colonel."

"I prefer a little more enthusiasm and involvement than that. Do you have your room key with you?"

"Yes, in my pocket—all right." He dropped it into the waiting palm and it was passed to the man beside the driver in the front seat. The car stopped and he got out. The car then went on, moving slowly down dark streets, the ready guns discouraging Tony from any attempt at escape.

"You will tell me what happened to the money."

"There seems to be a great deal of interest in that. It was taken by your associate Angus Macpherson and his henchman from the airfield. He was helped by a number of other thugs, looked like six at least, who jumped in when the car was stopped."

"Would you recognize these men again?"

"Angus and his buddy, sure, but Jorge here could do that as well as I could. As to the others—I might be able to. I had a good close look at a couple of them."

"Then I will need your co-operation to do just that. And I am guaranteeing that co-operation." The car stopped and the recently departed skyjacker climbed back in. Grinning broadly, he passed a sheaf of rustling bills to the colonel. They all, except Tony, smiled as well at this.

"Very good," the colonel said. "This is our little insurance of your co-operation. Do you recognize these?" These were a bundle of hundred dollar bills in a leather wallet that he revealed briefly, then returned to his inner jacket pocket.

"One guess? The skyjacked money Jorge took from the plane?"

"Precisely. A tiny part of the whole, which we *will* have back. Using your name and room number as identification, our compatriot has changed one of these bills in your hotel. It will soon be discovered that they are hot. You will be fingered—for does not one Latin look like any other to these pale Anglos?"

"I'm an Indian. An Apache."

"They cannot tell the difference. The police will seek you. Aid us in recovering the money and we will tell them what we did."

"Honestly, that is the most simple-minded plan I ever heard of. No one will ever think for a moment I'm really involved . . ." The gun ground deep into the sore gun-grinding spot in his side. "But I'll help you for other reasons. I'm convinced."

He slumped into the seat in black despair, watching the traffic whir by, firmly and strongheadedly, all going in the wrong direction.

When the car stopped next it was before a conservatively elegant house nestled into a tree-rich square. Colonel Juarez-Sedoño led the way and Tony was easily persuaded to follow. A liveried butler bowed them in and opened the door of a book-lined study for them. The colonel waved Tony to one leather armchair, then took another for himself. The butler brought a dusty bottle and two balloon glasses before leaving in silence and closing the doors.

"You see," the colonel said, examining the bottle closely with his good eye, "I treat you as a friend, keep nothing from you, welcome you into my home. And ask very little in return."

"You are asking a lot, Colonel, since I am a representative of the United States Government. It is my duty to report everything that occurs."

"And so you shall, my dear boy, as soon as this little adventure is over. When we have the money I shall close my home here and move to Spain, where the climate, both political and physical, is far more agreeable. You may then tell all you know. But for the moment you aid us. Tell your officials it was done under duress, they will never know differently. Do the right thing and, who knows, there may be a little numbered bank account for you in Switzerland with some money in it."

"Are you trying to bribe me?"

"Of course, doesn't everyone?" He seemed genuinely astonished at Tony's warm reaction. Tilting the bottle carefully, he poured golden fluid into the glasses. "This is a treat I know you will enjoy, I have so few bottles left. Pre-Castro Bacardi *añejo*, rum more delicate than the finest cognac. To the counter-revolution."

He raised his glass, although Tony did not return the toast, and they drank. It was heavenly stuff with a bouquet of flowers, warm as the Cuban sun on the tongue. The colonel held his nose over the rim of the glass and inhaled deeply, then rolled his eyes upward in silent pleasure.

"One day soon we will return to our homeland and free the simple peasants from the bondage of red criminal slavery. For this we need money, and to gain the money I permitted myself to become involved with an outlaw Gael by the name of Angus Macpherson. He presented me with a plan that appeared to be foolproof, and certainly was if we do not consider his betrayal, so with a certain reluctance I went along. You see how frank I am with you? We arranged the recent affair for the mutual bene-fit of our nationalistic parties, though he has been greedy and desires all the money for his own. Cuba shall not remain en-chained because of him! We leave soon for Glasgow to pick up his trail. There is a certain tobacconist that we used for a message drop and our search begins there."

Tony drank deep and received a refill. He thought the colonel was mad but decided against telling him so. Even the dimmest of Hebridian revolutionaries would know enough to close off any trails that might lead the Cubans to them. Nevertheless he would have to go along with their plans for the moment. Per-haps he could escape en route.

"Just how will we get to Glasgow?" he asked.

"We shall drive. One of the men is renting a car now. This cursed country is so small that stolen cars are worse than useless. The police are alerted almost instantly." There was a discreet knock at the door. "It is time to go. Take the rum, it will perhaps make a dull journey bearable."

There were some harsh words from the colonel when the rented car turned out to be a Volkswagen bus. There were apologetic explanations about the tourist season, nothing else available, it did have room for them all until, in the end, he slid the door wide, muttering darkly, and climbed in. Tony, urged on in a now familiar manner, was encouraged to follow. There were seven of them in all and their luggage consisted solely of four violin cases and an attaché case, undoubtedly full of ammunition for the violins. With a rattle and a great whir from the miniature power plant concealed somewhere between the back wheels, they were off.

They drove for the entire night. It was all very much of a blur to Tony, who, still fatigued by a sleepless night and upset circadian rhythms, managed to get a good portion of the bottle of rum inside of him until he slumped onto a padded latin shoulder and fell asleep. He was dimly aware of lights flashing by, traffic on a motorway, much Spanish cursing and argument when they lost their way—this happened more than once—and finally a gray dawn that brightened only slightly into a foggy morning. Other sleepers awoke and there were cries of pain until the driver stopped by a tall hedge where they all stood in a row while a fine rain spattered their heads. Then onward.

"Glasgow," the driver announced as the road lifted onto a bridge that spanned a slate-gray river.

"I'm hungry," Tony said suddenly as his waking stomach threw off the anesthesia of the alcohol and painfully called attention to itself.

"We cannot stop," the colonel announced. "Most of the men in this car are wanted by the police. We will go hungry for the glory of the counterrevolution."

"That has nothing to do with me," Tony said petulantly. "Or you for that matter, Colonel. That hot bill won't have reached the bank yet and no one knows we are involved in this thing."

"You are correct," the colonel said with instant military decision. "Drop us off at Central Station, where we will mix with the milling crowds and where strangers will not be noticed, and come back in a half an hour."

The colonel seemed to run a taut ship, or VW bus, when it

came to discipline, because, other than some rapidly vibrating eyebrows, there were no complaints about this state of affairs. The driver made a number of wrong turnings but eventually let them out next to a gloomy and imposing Victorian structure. Though it was only seven in the morning the station was bustling with Scotch life, as well as the visitors the colonel had mentioned. The colonel took Tony firmly by the arm and spoke gently into his ear.

"I am a perfect shot and I have a silenced revolver in my side pocket. Make any attempt to escape, any at all, and there will be a small poof of sound and you will be one with eternity. Understood?"

"Understood, understood. That is not the first time I have heard it recently, either. Look, Colonel, could we buy some newspapers to read with breakfast, you must be as interested as I am in the latest developments."

The colonel was. They purchased *The Times* and *The Scotsman* and entered a great glowing buffet rich with the odor of frying fish, cooking bacon, bubbling oatmeal and other northern gustatory delights. Tony forgot his troubles and stood on tiptoe to look over the shoulders to make his choice. The shoulders immediately ahead of him, broad and blue-coated, turned about as he bobbed expectantly and he found himself looking into the surprised face of Captain Sterling Haycroft, pilot of the skyjacked aircraft.

SEVEN

"What the devil are you doing here, Hawkin? I was told you were in London."

No ready response sprang forward instantly so Tony had to resort to an echoed version of the same question.

"Tubby told me you were with the aircraft and wouldn't leave."

"He was right. But the owners telegraphed me to co-operate with the police and sent out a guard with a police dog, some local outfit called Fangs and Truncheons, so I did what I was ordered. Looked at all the mug books in London, then they sent me up here to look at more pics the local police have. The night train just got in."

"Train?"

"Sure. You don't think I fly when I don't have to? And you?"

If Tony had not been thinking of a quick answer the colonel had. He leaned forward and smiled ingratiatingly at Haycroft.

"May I introduce myself. I am Juan Garcia, a Mexican national and an old friend of Tony's. When I read of his presence in the papers I instantly invited him to stay at my comfortable home. In a further attempt to relax his nerves I have brought him on a brief motoring holiday to Scotland and to visit a mutual acquaintance who is studying urological surgery at the university here. A pleasure to make your acquaintance."

"Likewise. I hope you have a good time." Haycroft turned and seized a tray, apparently taken in by the story. Tony felt an all too familiar jab in the side as the colonel spoke. "Take the tray, dear friend, for both of us. My hand is still sore from the bashing I took at cricket the other day at Lord's." For all his other faults the colonel did have a fertile imagination.

A whiff of bacon aroma brought Tony back to more pressing matters at hand. Haycroft was loading his tray and Tony did the same. A motherly woman behind the counter gave him a bowl of what he thought was oatmeal but she called porridge, forced a piece of fried fish upon him—you try a golden kipper, love, makes a perfect breakfast—some toast and a cup of tea black as a bowling ball. She doubled everything when the colonel indicated an appetite as well. The colonel paid, his one hand uninjured by cricket fishing out the money, and they had no choice but to follow Haycroft to a table. Even the hissed assurance that he would die instantly if he revealed anything did not interfere with Tony's appetite. They all gnashed and chomped well for a bit until Haycroft sighed, leaned back and lit a thin, dark cigar from a pack in his pocket.

"Nothing like a Scots breakfast to hold the ribs together. It will get me through a long day of looking at Hibernian criminals. What do the papers say about the case?"

"Haven't looked yet," Tony mumbled.

"The police found how the guns got aboard, or at least where they were. In one of the toilets. I locked it myself, in Karachi, thing went on the fritz. Turns out the wiring in the monomatic was sabotaged. Sometime after I locked it, and before we left, the weapons were sneaked in there and the thing relocked. That's their theory, probably right. With a little bribery you can get away with anything at the Eastern airports."

"The bribery is the way of life in my country as well," the colonel said, leaning forward, finding a topic close to his heart. "A bribe is referred to as a *mordida*, a little bite. The motto is '*No hay reglas fijas*,' which might be translated as there are no fixed rules, but is better expressed by saying if you can afford it you can get anything. Even murder is possible, a certificate of death by accident purchased before the act from the police is all that is needed."

"I don't doubt you for a second, Mr. Garcia, not for a second. I'm going to run, the quicker I look at the goon photos the quicker I get back."

A man of decision, he was up and gone in an instant. The colonel watched closely to see that he went out of the station, then waved Tony to his feet.

"Leave the rest," he ordered. "He may be suspicious, informing the police right now. We leave."

They did. A mud-splattered VW bus filled with scowling, unshaven and hungry Cubans picked them up as soon as they appeared, then shot quickly away when the colonel told them what had happened. Tony burped happily and they looked daggers at him. Jorge was driving now and he must have been on a mission here before because he knew his way quite well. They worked their way through ever-grubbier streets, crossed the river again, then plunged into a narrow road. Among the small shops located here was one with a weathered sign that read J. HARDY—TOBACCONIST. A weathered man, who might have been J. Hardy himself, was taking down a wooden shutter that covered his window. The VW whirred on by and around the next corner, where it stopped.

"Did you see the place?" the colonel asked. "And the man in front?" Tony nodded abstractedly, worried a piece of fish with his tongue, attempting to dislodge it from between his teeth. "That is the place. Hardy knows me, I have been there before, and no one else in this vehicle can talk English. With the exception of you. You will therefore go to this store—we will be watching with deadly guns trained, alert for any false move—and will order ten Players."

"What's a Player?"

"They are cigarettes and they come in packages of various sizes. You will say 'Packet of ten Players, please,' for that is the code word. Immediately after saying this you add 'Prince Charlie lives!' "

"Who is Prince Charlie?"

"If your ignorance of history is so abysmal it is not for me to attempt to alleviate it. Go now—and do not forget the guns."

Tony went. He had every intention of keeping on going, too. The information first, he must try to get that, but instantly afterward he had to try to give these Latin thugs the slip. There was an edge like dull razor blades to the wind that cut through his thin jacket, accompanied by a damp smell of rain hovering close. Did the sun ever shine here? When he opened the door a bell tinkled overhead and a tired woman came through a curtain from the rear. Most of the shelves in the shop were half empty, and what goods were there seemed uninteresting to anyone. Dusty pipes with tiny bowls, cans with labels turned away that he could not read, mysterious envelopes and packages. The only touch of color was a rotating holder on the counter with variegated postcards on it.

"Good morning," Tony said cheerily as he closed the door behind him. The woman looked him up and down with complete indifference and remained silent. "Brisk weather, though." Perhaps she was mute? He came closer and gazed down through the patina of scratches on the glass counter top through which there was reluctantly revealed the cigarettes below. "Packet of ten Mayors, please." She didn't move; that wasn't right. "I mean *Players.*"

This twanged some thin thread of communication because she bent and extracted a package of cigarettes and placed them on the glass between them. As soon as she had done this he whispered, *"Prince Charlie lives!"*

This elicited a gratifyingly fine reaction. Her head jerked up, her eyes flicked briefly to one side, then back again, and she spoke loudly over her shoulder. "John, front, John," as though calling a dog. Instead the weathered J. Hardy himself pushed through the curtain.

"Arrr," he said, or something that sounded like that.

"Gentleman wants ten Players."

"Give him."

She fluttered her hands, not knowing what else to say, so Tony came to the rescue. "I also said that Prince Charlie lives."

Hardy looked aside quickly, then back at Tony as he swept the cigarettes from the counter and put them back in the case. He had a deep and nasty voice.

"None of that here. No Players. Get out."

That took care of the information. Escape was still a possibility.

"All right, forget all that. Do you have a back door? Some friends, a joke, I'll go out by the rear."

The bell jingled merrily as Hardy spoke up, even louder. "No back door, out you, out the front and keep moving." They all jumped and turned when Colonel Juarez-Sedoño spoke up.

"Attempting to escape after all I told you? You will be sorry."

Tony was, instantly, as a painful blow to his kidney sent him reeling back against the counter. Four more of the Cubans pushed in and closed the door, crowding the tiny store. The colonel took a wallet out of his jacket and spread some newspaper clippings from it proudly on the counter, pushing them forward, smiling up at the man and woman beyond.

"This man will be killed and left here. You will perhaps be killed too. Read these, they are in English. Note the heading 'Batista Butcher Flees Cuba' and the fine picture of myself below it. And this one of gunned-down corpses, and read below of statements of prisoners about obscene tortures. All of this is true."

As though to add punctuation he slapped Tony hard across the face, sending him staggering backward; strong hands pushed him to the counter again. The suave gentleman was gone, replaced by the cold torturer. The newspaper reports had to be true. Tony recognized that instantly. As did the tobacconist and his wife, who were obviously terrified. The colonel smiled, without warmth, at this recognition of his abilities—took his gun from his pocket and pressed its cold muzzle to Tony's temple.

"Shall I blow this man's brains across the interior of your filthy establishment to convince you? Tell me where I can find the people who used to leave messages for me."

"We know . . . nothing." Hardy's voice trembled.

"Oh yes you do. They told you to shut up, to cease all messages. But you know where they are and you are going to tell me. After this man is dead I kill your wife." The hammer made a sinister click as he cocked the gun. Tony spoke up loudly:

"Wait! They told me something, at least they reacted when I gave them the password. Each of them looked in *that* direction very quickly, then looked back."

Inevitably they all turned. There was nothing of importance or interest to see. Just the dusty corner of the shop and the rack of postcards.

"Of course," the colonel said, and lowered the gun. "A postcard. A location. A simple form of communication. This is your only chance, Hardy, your *only* chance—do you understand? Hesitate for one instant and I kill this man to prove to you that I do mean what I say. Hesitate for an instant more and your wife is dead. It goes without saying that you will be killed as well. And all for nothing. To protect a ragtag band of simpletons. Now, make your mind up and get ready."

In the brief silence he put the gun back to Tony's head. The men holding him stepped aside so as not to be behind him. This, as much as anything the colonel had said, was assurance that he was ready to commit cold-blooded murder at any time.

"GIVE ME THE POSTCARD!"

The words were a roared command. Tony jumped as though he had been shot already, feeling this was his last moment on earth.

Hardy grabbed a postcard from the rack and threw it on the counter.

"Very good," the colonel said, lowering the gun and putting the card into his pocket without looking at it. "Before we leave be sure in your heart that you have given me the correct card because I will not come back and ask you again. If it is wrong there will be shots from the darkness at night and you both will be dead meat. Just nod your head, do not speak—it *is* the correct card?"

Both of the terrified people nodded dumbly and Tony hated this man for the humiliation they had all suffered at his hands. He would never forget it. Quietly he vowed that, if and when he got out of this mess, he would see a little justice directed in the colonel's direction.

"That was simple enough," the colonel said as they strolled back to the car, the perfect gentleman again. "I thought they would see light when they saw how expendable a traitor could be."

He was a beast, Tony realized, but a dangerously intelligent one. Everything had been planned from the beginning, including Tony's attempt to escape. He had been outmaneuvered right down the line. Even now the colonel was smiling as he looked at Tony's face, laughing, knowing just what thoughts were going through his mind. Tony turned away and entered the bus.

"Now, where is this place?" The colonel seated himself comfortably and held the card up to the light and the intense gaze of his single eye. "Fishing boats, a harbor, very attractive. And the name, Carradale—the Jewel of Argyll. How very poetic. Find me this Argyll on the map."

There was much rattling of paper and muttering and mispronunciation in Spanish before the spot was found. "Here," Jorge announced proudly. "On this peninsula by a big island. We must take the road number eighty-two to the north, and then the road eighty-three to the south. A drive of perhaps one hundred and thirty miles."

"We go there. Begin."

"But, Colonel, hunger tears at our vitals with sharp teeth. Can we not now eat?"

"Possibly. Drive on. We will stop at a shop and I will buy provisions. You can eat while we drive. There, halt by that market and I will provide for you."

He returned quickly with two large bags, which he opened as soon as they had moved on, displaying his purchases proudly. "The pork pie, very delicious when taken with mustard, and most filling. Simply bite and eat. And the sausage roll. Little flavor but equally filling. It is not the hour for the purchase of alcoholic beverages yet, you know the British eccentricity in this matter, but here is milk in bottles, much more nourishing."

They champed happily. Tony looked on with eagerness but, perhaps because of his recent meal, was offered nothing. It began to rain and Tony's morale stayed at rock bottom. Would he get out of this alive? There was no telling, or rather there was telling. If the colonel thought he had information best kept secret there would be a quick bullet, he had no doubt of that. So what he had to do was appear frightened—he didn't have to fake that—and co-operate instantly when anything was asked of him. Willing and able. But all the time he must be alert for the chance to escape from these dangerous men. Not an obvious escape, the colonel would be as aware as he was of anything like that. In fact he must ignore the obvious in the hopes of getting the colonel ever so slightly off his guard. Nevertheless his eyes must be open and his brain seething with inquiry, examining everything. When the opportunity presented itself he had to seize it upon the instant and be gone.

All this fervid thinking had a slightly ameliorating effect on his morale, which the appearance of the sun helped considerably. The rain had ceased, the clouds rolled back and slanting rays of light poked down like heavenly fingers. The road was a narrow track that wound between stone-walled fields. Grass that was green enough to hurt the eye filled the meadows, where it was being happily grazed by great, white, barrel-shaped sheep. They lifted black faces to the car as it went by, chewing placidly, at peace with the world. This world was at peace with itself and the knot of armed and desperate men rushing through it was the sour note. Plantations of fir swept by, purple and yellow flowers blossomed on the hillsides, small farms trickled smoke upward from their chimneys into the utterly transparent air. Tony forgot his predicament in the beauty of it, glimpses of ocean between the hills, sea gulls floating overhead. It was an incredibly lovely landscape. The road wound up, between and around the hills, darted down through tiny villages only to climb the next slope on the other side. All, except the driver, enjoyed the scenery; he was too busy rowing up and down the hills with the gear shift, getting the most out of the laboring engine. The road improved going through Inveraray, but soon after resumed its normal looping and soaring.

It was then that the first Cuban, stuffed with meat pies and milk and assaulted by the vibration of the car, admitted to an increase in internal pressure. Others chimed in in agreement until they convinced the colonel that another halt was in order. The driver slowed and, after a good deal of shouted discussion about the precise locale for the function, pulled off onto the grass where the road made a loop around the base of a small hill. There was a stand of birch trees here, their trunks white against the dark forest that marched up over the rise of the steeper hill beyond. It was an idyllic spot, silent and calm, with the smooth waters of Kilbrannan Sound close by beyond the road. Tony looked out at it with appreciation until the colonel tugged on his arm.

"You, too, out."

"But I don't feel I want to . . ."

"That was an order, not a request," the colonel answered in his own sweetly obnoxious way.

Tony grumbled and followed the rest of them across the resilient softness of the grass to the trees beyond. The others were all close-by, there was not a weapon in sight—and he realized exactly what he had to do. Stroll in among the trees, stroll a bit farther, ever so slowly. But at the first shout of attention he began running, straight into the grove.

It was a simple plan and had the advantage of surprise, and he was dodging even deeper among the trunks before the pursuit even began. One shot was fired that thudded into a tree nearby; the colonel's order stopped all firing. They wanted him alive. He had hoped they would, which meant that they would then have to catch him on foot. This proved the case. He pushed through the brush, ducking under low-hanging limbs, going as fast as he could, while behind him came mixed shouts and crashings. None of his captors had been expecting his escape and, in more ways than one, they were caught with their pants down.

A wall appeared ahead, flat stones laid one on top of the

other, and he scrambled up this desperately, slipping on the moss that covered it, then hurled himself into the meadow on the other side—almost landing on a large and fat sheep. This fled, baaing in fear, an accompanying lamb maaing in concert. Through the field Tony ran, or rather up it, for it was a hillside field and steep enough to make the going difficult. Well if it was difficult for him it was just as difficult for the skyjackers; press on! His heart was thundering with the effort, a red haze of fatigue clouding his eyes, lungs gasping for air by the time he reached the wall at the top. He felt he could not go on a moment longer, yet he knew he had to. With scratching fingers he clawed his way to the top of the fence, then glanced behind before he fell heavily on the other side.

The Cubans were spread out unevenly across the meadow, the slowest just climbing the lower fence, the swiftest halfway up and being urged on by the colonel, who stood on the fence below and called to them for greater efforts. He must press on!

Or must he? Hadn't Old Fred, pride of the FBI, provided him with the answer to a situation like this? He had indeed! Tony bent and pulled strongly at his heel—and nothing happened. Wasn't this the heel with the mini-grenades in it? Or perhaps it was the other one. Angry Spanish curses were gasped from the field beyond the fence as he scratched at the other shoe. The heel promptly opened and dumped the grenades out onto the ground.

Pull the pin on top, right. Perhaps they did not want to kill him, but the feeling was not necessarily mutual. He looked over the fence again and saw the first man no more than thirty feet away. With a sharp pull he ripped the pin free and threw the small grenade in a high arc.

Off to one side. In the last instant he realized he could not kill any of the skyjackers in cold blood, as much as they probably deserved it.

Despite its size the grenade went off with a satisfying boom, sending clods of dirt flying in all directions. In the instant every man in the field was flat on his face, cries of outrage signifying that more than one of them had found that a sheep meadow was not the ideal place for this activity. Tony jumped to the top of the fence and waved another grenade over his head, shouting angrily:

"Death to the counterrevolution!"

This explosion was even closer to the men, raining dirt on some of them, and their response was most satisfying. Despite the orders of the colonel, they all fled back down the hill to the safety of the fence. A third grenade kept them moving. He shoveled the remaining grenades into his pocket, grinning happily.

Ducking low so he could not be seen from below, Tony moved as swiftly as he could back into the shelter of the pine trees. He straightened up as soon as they were thick enough and walked uphill as steadily and as fast as he could. They would have no way of knowing he was gone, and by the time they did get up enough nerve to try and cross the field again he would be well away. Success!

Only what did he do next? So far he had just fled by reflex. Now that he had broken contact with the enemy he had to keep it that way, while at the same time working out some plan. The countryside seemed empty of habitation—and there was only the single road. That was clue enough—he had to stay away from the road, at least for the time being, for they were sure to keep it under observation. But without the road where could he go? Nowhere. Perhaps he might just stay in the trees, stay out of sight until they gave up the chase and left. But this might take a good while and although the weather had been fine lately, it could change. As though to remind him of this, thunder rumbled ominously in the distance and a cloud passed in front of the sun. No thank you. He wasn't dressed for this kind of an exercise, not in a lightweight suit that became lighter every moment as the wind cut through it to his sweat-damp skin. He shivered and climbed faster.

When he reached the brow of the hill the forest stopped and a smooth slope of low plants and bushes swooped downward in a valley toward the sea beyond. He stayed furtively among the trees but was not able to see enough until he crouched and crawled through the bushes to the edge of the slope. Far below, beside the road, was a neat white farmhouse. Wires ran to it from a pole at the edge of the road, electricity undoubtedly, telephone perhaps. With a decided click that echoed in his frontal lobes his mind decided on a positive course of action.

Telephone. It would mean calling the police, 999, he even remembered the number to dial, which would probably mean arrest on the hot money charge. He could get out of that, the FBI would find a way and, no matter how uncomfortable he would be as a jailbird, it was far superior to nipping about the Scotch Highlands with murderous Cuban gunmen on his heels. The house it would be.

He started to rise—then instantly sat again. No. As clearly as though he were seeing it projected on a screen, he saw himself walking into the colonel's unwelcome embrace. This was too obvious and the colonel would be expecting it. The farmhouse was out. Something more subtle, and strenuous, was in order. He could not, *must* not, take the obvious course. He had to carry on, up the steep slope through the trees to the highest point, then down the other side. Anything less would be as good as surrendering to the colonel.

Soaked with sweat, dampened by a sudden rainstorm, stumbling with fatigue, he reached the summit of the hill, which now had assumed Everestian proportions, and dropped with a trembling sigh onto a handy boulder. On all sides the slopes fell away from him and, through the thin rank of trees, he could see the waters of the Sound on three sides. The hill obviously formed a small peninsula projecting into the sea, with the road skirting its base. To escape from the peninsula he must turn right and walk back through the rising hills inland. This seemed the obvious course, the only intelligent one, so he vowed not to follow it. That way the minions of the colonel undoubtedly lurked. To be completely irrational he should go to the left, down the hill to the tip of the peninsula, from which the only escape would be by sea or road. This was so impractical that he knew at once he must do it. He had no idea what he would find there—and neither did the colonel. It was the only course open to him. If no possibility of escape then offered itself he could always hide in the trees until dark, then try to make his way out by road, get a lift from a car, find a friendly farmhouse, anything. This was what he had to do.

Going downhill was harder than climbing up and he had to stop often to rest. He wished now that he had led a cleaner life lately, worked out in the gym every day, lost a few pounds, kept regular hours, got the old muscle tone back. But he hadn't. Sighing deeply, he stumbled on. When he was almost three quarters of the way down, the land fell away in a sudden cliff. Concealed by this formation up until now, a small building presented itself by the side of the road, just on the tip of the peninsula. It was solidly built and charming, flowers growing at its walls, a sign of some sort on its side. There were no trees here but plenty of shelter from the shrubbery as long as he stayed low. With great care he went down the slope until he could read the sign. HIGH-LAND HANDICRAFTS. That sounded nice. A tourist shop of some kind, people inside used to hearing the strange accents of foreigners, certainly a telephone for commercial contact with the world outside. But should he risk it? The colonel could have no idea he had come this way, not over the entire mountain, well, hill. Was it a chance he should take?

As though he had asked the colonel himself the colonel answered. Around the hill below, buzzing with unleashed Teutonic mini-power, the VW bus came. It was going flat out, top speed, tires squealing as it negotiated the turn. Past the Highland Handicrafts without slowing, around the turn again, where it buzzed away out of sight. Now was the time, before it could come back —if it were coming back. The colonel was obviously checking both sides of the hill and had never considered the far end at all. Stumbling and sliding, Tony made it to the road with a rush. Brushing the worst of the leaves and debris from his clothing, he went to the door and opened it cautiously. There was no one inside. Still as carefully, ready as a frightened doe to retreat to the hills, he edged inside.

There were some very attractive paintings and prints on the wall that instantly caught his attention. No! He was an FBI man at this moment, not a dealer in fine art. Nevertheless he admired the handcrafted jewelry, the stoneware and weaving. By the windows, facing the road, was a desk with a handsome white-haired woman behind it.

"Good afternoon," she said. "May I help you?" He turned and saw the telephone by her elbow.

"Yes, good afternoon, you certainly can."

Smiling victoriously, he sauntered across the room between the fishing rods and cases of ornaments, rubbing his hands together. Success was his!

"You are late," a voice said behind him. "I didn't think your stroll would take so much time."

A puppet on a string, Tony spun about to face the smiling colonel, who stood in an alcove where he could not be seen from either the window or the door. He was reading a book, which he lowered just long enough to show Tony the silenced revolver he held beneath it. Then he strolled over to stand close behind him.

"You naughty chap. You know we must be going. Here, I know your tastes, I am sure this is what you want." He took a toy sheep from the counter and handed it to Tony. It rested on his hand, empty glass-bead eyes staring into his from under curled horns made from pipe cleaners, fuzzy rabbit fur for wool, black wooden legs peeking out below. "I'll even pay for it. Now we must be going."

"Good-bye, sir," the proprietress said cheerily, ringing up the sale. "Those sheep are nice, aren't they? Made by a local girl, does everything herself."

When the door closed behind them the colonel ground the gun viciously into Tony's already sore side where guns had been ground before.

"You stupid fool. If I did not need you I would shoot you here and now. I will next time . . . I lose my patience. Now walk along the road until the car comes back. Your pathetic attempt at escape has not only earned you nothing but has raised my anger. Beware! Now, we are out of sight of the building, hands in the air—higher. Do you have more of the grenades?" The gun emphasized the question and Tony decided that lying was out of the question.

"In my pocket, I'll . . ."

"No you won't! Just stand where you are until the car gets here." It arrived all too quickly and Tony was brusquely and efficiently searched, the grenades transferred to one of the violin cases. Shoved and insulted, he was hurried back into the VW and the trip resumed. The road wound on through Tarbert, and a few miles farther on they turned off on a smaller road that followed the Sound that led to Carradale.

"We will be there soon, and no more foolish games from you," the colonel said, tracing their course on the map with a well-manicured finger. "When we arrive you, Jorge, will park the car and stay with it. I will stroll about the town with this creature Hawkin, who will be looking at faces and will co-operate with me or he will be loathsomely dead before the day is out. While we do this the rest of you will stroll as well, keeping us always in sight, but staying apart as though simple tourists here for a day's outing, wandering musicians with your instruments ready to play at a moment's notice. Guard my back at all times and beware of suspicious circumstances. Always remember the gun in my pocket, Hawkin. I will use it if I have to."

Over a hump-backed bridge and through meadows and forests the road twisted, then straightened out and widened as it reached the few shops that made up the village center. The colonel took it all in with his Cyclops eye.

"A butcher, nothing there, general goods, post office—there! The hotel, sure to contain a bar and a bar possibly to contain those we seek. Stop next to it."

"We'll have to order a drink to appear natural," Tony hinted.

"A single whisky, no more. Inside."

Inside was a long room with a dart board at one end, being industriously punctured by two elderly men with arthritic, palsied fingers. They blinked moistly at the newcomers, then turned back to their more interesting game, plunking the darts into the target numbers with incredible ease. Youth was also catered to by a pinball machine that was tinkling and clunking steadily under the attentions of an adenoidal, spotty teen-ager. Between these extremes lay the bar, where a half-dozen men were downing large glasses of beer. Tony looked at them closely; he recognized none of them. "Not here," he murmured.

"Two whiskies," the colonel ordered, standing so his shoulders were near the wall, his eyes upon the room. A young, exceedingly pink girl behind the bar took two wine glasses and pressed them each in turn up under a bottle of scotch secured upside down to the wall. A windowed device on the neck measured out an infinitesimal amount of drink into each glass. The colonel paid, their drinks vanished in a single small gulp, then they were back on the road again.

"We shall stroll down to the harbor there. Look carefully at everyone."

A jetty closed off one side of the circular harbor and two fishing boats were tied up to it. The sun shone brightly on this very pleasant scene, tiny cottages crouched along the shore, nets dried on poles, a small shop displayed rope and tackle in its window. The colonel inclined his head in that direction.

"In this store, eyes open."

There were big men there in rubber boots and heavy sweaters; they looked up in interest when they entered. Tony was sure he had never seen them before. "Can I help you, gentlemen?" the man behind the wooden counter asked. Also a stranger. The colonel looked around quickly at the wrenches, cans of grease and red lead—then saw a rack of paperback books.

"Yes, something to read." He flipped through them unseeingly, eyes on Tony, who gave his head a quick shake. The colonel threw a small booklet on the counter, it was nearest to hand. "I'll take this."

"That'll be twenty-five pence."

Colonel Juarez-Sedoño passed it to Tony while he dug in his pocket for silver. There was a dim and watery seascape on the front cover of the booklet, fishing boats emerging from a cove, with the title below. "THE FLEET and other poems" by Ian A. Brown. The colonel was having difficulty fishing out small change and Tony flipped the pages. "A la Cart" sounded like a nice title for a poem:

> Herring swimming in Loch Fyne
> feed on plankton in the brine;
> those seen on the surface frying
> soon inside a net are lying;
> then may this simple fish
> fried in meal—a tasty dish!

A very nice poem that set Tony's salivary glands to secreting and brought an answering mutter of interest from his stomach. It had been a long time since he had eaten. The colonel tugged at his arm.

"Along the shore, look at the men on the boats."

They ambled over to the water's edge, while in the background simple Cuban musicians strolled as well, violin cases hanging heavy from their hands. A man was gutting a large fish on the deck of the nearest boat, throwing the waste parts into the water where gulls screamed and fought for the tidbits. He looked up when they came close and Tony recognized the driver of the Rolls-Royce, the man who had helped Angus Macpherson take the money. Tony turned away and spoke softly:

"That's one of them, the driver of the car."

The colonel smiled broadly and took the gun from his pocket.

"Come here, you," he ordered.

The sailor responded instantly by hurling his knife at the colonel.

EIGHT

For all his skill as a torturer, the colonel was not much of a combat specialist. He neither fired his gun nor attempted to dodge, but simply shrieked shrilly as the knife lodged in his thigh, flinging his arms wide and falling backward, sending the gun flying across the cobbles. The shrieking cut off as he crashed to the ground, his eyes rolling up so only the whites showed, his mouth lolling open. The knife fell from his leg with the impact and a small splotch of blood stained the spot where it had gone in. His jacket had fallen open, and there, projecting from the inner pocket, was the wallet with the skyjacked bills peeping greenly from it.

There would never be another chance like this—and Tony took it. The fish cleaner had vanished from the boat while startled Cubans were still fumbling with violin case closures. Now! Grabbing the wallet from the colonel's pocket, Tony raced across the cobbles and into an alleyway next to the store. There was a path here that rose sharply up the hillside. He thrust the wallet into his pocket and scrabbled up it, almost on all fours. There was only silence from the harbor behind him and he risked a quick look over his shoulder. None of the Cubans were in sight—but the knife wielder from the boat was coming up the path behind him.

There is nothing like a quick whiff of fear to flush out the adrenals and start the heart pumping. Tony whirred up the steep side of the hill, arms and legs churning like windmills, between the houses at the top toward the beckoning road beyond. A sturdy young man came out of one of the houses and looked at him with interest. Tony slowed to a walk and tried to think of something inconsequential to say. Before he could open his mouth his pursuer called out:

"Hold him, Bruce, he's one of them from the plane."

Bruce's reactions were not the quickest. He frowned in thought and Tony pushed by him, then reluctantly made his mind up at the last possible instant. A large hand reached out and seized Tony's jacket and that was that. He struggled fiercely but to no avail, and was drawn in steadily like the Loch Fyne herring of the poem. His grinning pursuer came quickly up and the two of them had no trouble in forcing Tony through the door into the building. It closed behind him with a very final sound. They were in a large, beamed kitchen. A short man with sandy hair and steel-rimmed thick glasses looked up from the table where he was drinking a cup of tea. "What's this?" he asked quietly.

"This one is from the plane, the American FBI man. He came to town with a whole shoal of those Cubans. One of them showed me a gun and I stuck him in the leg. Where's Angus?"

"In the parlor with the fencing-cully. We can't bother him now."

"What's to do?"

"Do nothing until we ask Angus. He won't be long—"

The sharp cracking sound of two pistol shots from behind the door came as punctuation to his sentence. Once more the knife thrower from the boat showed the speed of his reflexes for, as the others stood gaping, he jumped forward and hurled himself against the door. It creaked loudly—but held fast. As he struck it again a car started up in the road outside, tires spinning and squealing as it roared away. The door crashed open to reveal Angus Macpherson lying face down on the floor, beyond him the open front door.

In this still moment Tony struggled to get free. But the stolid Bruce was the perfect captor. He had been ordered to hold, and hold he did, gaping into the parlor and scarcely aware of Tony's writhing. They were bending over Angus now, looking up with shocked faces.

"He's dead, stone dead, Willy. What are we to do?"

"Don't panic," the sandy-haired man said, stroking his heavy glasses in thought. "Close the street door. Get the others in here. The money's gone, isn't it?"

"By God yes! He's killed poor Angus and taken it all."

Willy looked up and saw Tony, then pointed a quick finger in his direction. "Get that one out of here for now. Lock him in the pantry."

Muscled arms forced Tony across the room and through a low wooden door. It crashed shut behind him and he could hear a heavy bolt being slid into place. He was in a small room lined with shelves, mostly empty, and lit by a small barred window in the wall. The door was thick, he found that out when he pressed his ear to it; all he could hear was tantalizing murmurs of sound from the other room. All right, what about the window—if he was going to escape now was the time while the confusion was at its highest. When he stood on the shelves his shoulders were level with the window. It had no glass in it but was covered by a rusty piece of screen that came away when he touched it—to reveal heavy iron bars set in a solid metal frame. Now what? While he was considering that a man ran by outside shouting to someone unseen.

"A green Capri, it was. Number 8463Y. Went by me like a bat from hell."

The car—what else! The murderer and the money. What was the number—8463Y? He was never going to remember it. Going through his pockets he found nothing to write with, nor was there anything other than a bundle of hundred dollar bills in the colonel's wallet. There was a bent nail on the window sill and he used this to scratch a message onto the end of the uppermost bill. GRN—CAPRI—8463Y. Done. Now to get out of here. And on his wrist the means of escape. Praise be for the good old FBI know-how.

When he pulled the tape off his wrist it took bits of skin with it, good tape that, and the wire length of the gigli saw fell free. He did not know how long it would take to saw through the bars but the sooner he started the quicker he would be out of here. Carefully he slid one end around the center bar and retrieved it. His index fingers fitted neatly into the loops at the ends of the wire saw so he could draw it taut against the metal. When he pulled it back and forth it instantly sank through the layers of paint and rust and chewed at the solid iron. Wonderful!

He worked it back and forth quickly a half-dozen times and the saw broke in half.

Looking at the dangling lengths of wire, he felt only a great rage rising within him. It would have worked—it should have worked! But it broke. Why? Why anything, why this whole mad business? Wanting to lash out at something, he kicked the wall, but this only hurt his toe. Still possessed by anger, he seized the bars and pulled at them with all his might. They did not budge in the slightest.

Disgustedly he pushed them from him. The frame grated free from its loose lodging in the brick wall and fell heavily to the ground outside.

So much for fancy FBI techniques. Without questioning he accepted this windfall instantly and hurled himself through the window, banging his knee badly, then skinning his shin as he squeezed through and slithered to the ground outside. There was no one in sight and, before any more of the muscled men could appear, he limped quickly up the road. As he came to the turning below the town center he heard a familiar coffee grinder whir from below and had plenty of time to seek cover in a sheltering doorway before the laboring VW bus churned slowly by. Worried faces were at every window with ready gun muzzles peeping shyly from below. None of the faces was that of the colonel, who, unless deserted on the cobbles of the harbor, must be lying, still unconscious, in the bus. The penalty of over-centralization of authority; all the lackeys could do was retire and regroup and wait for him to regain control. Passed out with fear when he had been pinked by the knife! The memory of that warmed Tony and was balm to his aches as he hurried up the hill in the wake of the vanished VW. A coward and a bully, not to mention a sadist, that is what the good colonel was. Eager to dish it out, petrifying with fear when on the receiving end. He would be twice the vicious enemy now that his little secret was known—but it was surely a secret worth knowing. Tony wished there was some way he could communicate the truth to the weathered J. Hardy and wife.

With a last heaving grade the road flattened out in the village center. All was as it should be here; apparently news of the events in the harbor and on the hillside below had not reached this far yet. Sturdy housewives emerged from stores with their laden wicker shopping baskets, calling cheerily one to the other; stalwart male Scots emerged from the bar calling out even more cheerily. One muscular man in blue coveralls—weren't there any runts or culls in this town?—stamped over to a red gravel truck that stood in the parking lot and climbed in. The engine snorted to life and he backed out. ROBINSON, BUILDERS the legend on the door read. Tony had to stand clear as it swung out into the narrow road, going slowly to get by the parked cars, and for an instant the great tailgate hovered before him.

At times a nod is as good as a wink and here were nod and wink tapping him strongly on the shoulder. He did not need to be nodded, tapped or winked at twice. A quick glance around —no one was looking in his direction—then he clutched the grimy metal and hauled himself up and over to fall to the truck bed inside. There was a pile of loose rock forward that obscured the rear window to the driver's compartment; the sides were high enough to shield him from outside view. He lay back comfortably on the hard steel and watched the green boughs float by overhead.

Before they had gone more than a quarter of a mile there was a loud and imperious honking from behind the truck and his heart leapt like a rabbit over a hedge. Was he discovered? The truck was slowing, pulling over. . . .

There was the clatter of gravel thrown by spinning wheels as the anxious car pulled by and rushed ahead, the truck following cetaceously in its wake. After this there were no more alarms.

When the truck rose up and dropped again, then halted, Tony tried to recall the road as he had seen it when they had first come here. A car whirred by ahead of them and the truck started up, turning. A road junction and a hump-backed bridge where they had turned off. The truck was going left now which meant it was not going back, retracing the VW's track in reverse, but continuing instead farther down the road along the peninsula. To where? He had vague memories of the map and of something farther on, stronger memories of the fact that the peninsula ended soon and there was nothing but green Atlantic after that. A seaport perhaps? Visions of ferry boats danced in his head. Or would that be asking too much? Best to wait and see. He was safe enough and comfortable enough where he was for the time being. Well, at least safe enough. With unexpected speed white clouds had rushed up to cover the sun, then covered the sky and proceeded to produce a fine, chill and penetrating mist. He clutched his collar tight about his neck and shivered, droplets beading his face. His lightweight suit, perfect for a Washington muggy spring, offered little resistance to the weather of this northern latitude. He remembered, unhappily, a geography teacher who had pointed out that the northern parts of the British Isles, where he undoubtedly was right now, were located at the same latitude as Hudson's Bay in Canada. Only the beneficent Gulf Stream made them habitable. Where was the Gulf Stream now when he needed it? Ice floes and snow; it could be no colder in Hudson's Bay at this moment.

Only hell is said to last forever and even purgatory has its end. After an unmeasurable period of misery, first houses then taller red-brick buildings began to swim into view above him, while the toot of a distant horn announced that traffic was about. He didn't know where he was, but he had arrived. Anywhere at all was fine; he had to get out of the truck. When it slowed to a halt he raised his head up warily and saw a circular patch of green with a stone cross in the center of it, shining wet pavement all around. Under him the truck shuddered as it ground into gear and lurched forward. He was over the tailgate and in the road, and in two steps was on the grass. The elderly driver of a small car just behind the truck was looking at him in what might be taken to be a suspicious manner, so he turned and waved cheerily to the vanishing truck. The car followed the truck and both rolled out of sight down a side street. Tony walked over and appeared to be examining the cross with great enthusiasm but, instead, was trying to see just where chance had put him down.

Waves slapped against the sea wall on the other side of the road, the sea itself reflecting the slate-gray clouds that rushed by low overhead, dropping a bit of rain on their way. No ferrets here, just some fishing boats tied up farther along—and he was staying away from fishing boats, thank you. Walking about the cross he saw a mainish sort of street extending away from him with signs proclaiming stores of all kinds—even a five-and-ten and a supermarket. Civilization again! He stepped off the curb, then pulled his foot back again. No, don't look that way—look *this* way. This way showed two cars and three bicycles bearing down upon him and he waited until they were past before hurrying across. Nearest to hand was the establishment of W. Urquhart & Co.—Gentlemen's Haberdashers. That was more like it. He pushed open the door wearily and stumbled inside. It was warm and a smiling young lady stepped forward and asked him if there was anything she could do for him. He swept the stock with eager eyes and pointed to a woolly tweed cap on a plaster head.

"A cap, I would very much like a cap."

"Do you know your size, sir?"

"Seven, something like that."

"Why don't you try this one for size? . . . Fits fine, sir, very nice it is too. That's a good buy at ninety-five pence."

Pence? Pence. The land of pound and pence, he had forgotten about that. A quick glimpse into his thin wallet revealed a few singles and a solitary ten dollar bill, which he offered with an ingratiating smile to the girl. She looked at it, head cocked to one side, without a great deal of interest.

"I'm sorry, but we don't take foreign money here. Manager's orders. But the bank is just across the road. Closing in five minutes, and they can cash it for you."

Five minutes! "Fine, just what I'll do, I'll be right back." He opened the door and her warm voice, with ever so slight a cutting edge, came after him:

"You wouldn't like to leave the cap, would you, sir? I'll have it ready for you when you come back."

"Cap? Of course, I forgot. Here, I'll be right back."

He slunk out, sweating in the cold rain, almost grabbed as a felon, a sly cap thief. Looking both ways quickly to make sure the road was clear, he hurried across the street and up the bank steps where a man in a blue uniform was just shutting the door. For a long moment he looked somberly at Tony, then up at the clock, which still lacked two minutes of half-past three, sighed and reluctantly opened to admit him. The interior was all brown wood and brass and had a very nineteenth-century air about it. But telephones still worked, even if they were hand cranked, and word must have been spread by now of the ransom money. With trepidation he approached the window labeled FOREIGN EXCHANGE and wondered just what to do. The few dollars he had were not going to get him very far. But if he cashed any of the money from the colonel's wallet he risked apprehension by the police. Well—let them arrest him! He might be able to get out of the charges, he surely had to get out of the charges—they couldn't believe he really had anything to do with the skyjacking. And if he were arrested at least he would be safely away from hulking Hibernians and Cuban killers. Be bold!

"I would like to cash one hundred U.S. dollars," he said to the pallid creature imprisoned by the bars. "No, two—three hundred." Whatever the amount the crime would be the same.

"Just a moment, if you please, I have to check."

The teller left the window and went to confer with a colleague while Tony's heart did the now familiar triphammer routine inside his rib cage. The bank employees examined a sheet of paper, shook their heads sorrowfully over it, then the teller returned. A list of the stolen bills? The man looked very unhappy.

"You realize, sir, that there may be difficulties."

"Difficulties?" Why was his voice so high pitched?

"You know how it is, international finance and all that. Your dollar, if you will excuse my saying so, tends to go up and down a good deal. Usually down. One has to be sure of the current rate. It's down again," he added with insular relish.

"Whatever you say, here are the bills."

After much pencil scratching and rapid work with a hand-turned calculator the teller reached a conclusion and began to count bills out onto the counter before him. He was just adding coins to this when his associate came over and whispered in his ear, looking coldly at Tony all the while. The triphammer worked overtime.

"Sorry, sir," the teller said, not sounding sorry at all. "But it's gone down again." He pulled some of the bills from the pile and counted the rest again carefully.

He had done it! The guard, seeing now that he was a man of some substance and wealth despite his clothes, smiled and opened the door for him. While Tony had been in the bank the clouds had been whipped away and the cheerful sunlight reflected from the damp pavement and the puddles. When he strolled up, the girl in the haberdashers opened the door for him and he looked beyond her to the racks and drawers.

"Do you have raincoats?" he asked. She arched her eyebrows at this—does the Sahara have sunglasses?—and pointed to a heavily laden rack.

"We do a fine line of raincoats, sir. What sort would you like?"

This opportunity to stave off pneumonia and improve his appearance was too good to miss. A gray knitted sweater—was it really spring here?—a clean shirt along with a tweed tie to match his cap, a package of handkerchiefs and a change of underwear. Life was looking better.

"They lost my luggage," he explained. "Never caught up with me."

"Happened to my mother in Edinburgh."

With this gratuitous commiseration working for him he used the changing room to do just that while she added up his purchases. He paid gladly from inside his waterproof and woolly womb. "You don't have a razor, soap, you know?"

"Just along here at the chemists, they'll have what you need."

"I'll do that. And could you tell me, I know it sounds funny but you lose track, you know this is Monday so it must be Rome sort of thing, but—where am I?"

"In Urquhart, haberdashers," she responded briskly.

"No, I mean—what *city?*"

Most of the warmth was gone from her voice now. "Campbeltown, Argyll." Then, as an afterthought as she closed the door quickly after him, "That's in Scotland." Her eyes widened in fear and she stepped back a pace when she saw his foot was holding the door open. He clutched the paper bag of discarded clothes to him and attempted a friendly smile.

"I was pretty sure I was in Scotland. I even drove here with friends from Glasgow. But I have to hurry back. Could you tell me where the train station is?"

"No train here, none at all. The Duke of Argyll never liked trains." She was frightened. "But there is the plane to Glasgow. Afternoon flight leaves in ten minutes." The door closed firmly as he removed his foot.

Plane! Too good to be true. But ten minutes—where was the airport? And how was he to get there? He looked around wildly and saw trundling slowly towards him, like the answer to a secret wish, a stubby black car with the single word TAXI glowing on its roof. When he waved his arm it swung neatly up to the curb beside him.

"Can you take me to the airport?"

The driver, wearing a cloth cap very much like his, peered out at him through a great wealth of curling beard that merged into bushy sideburns. Hair even sprouted on the tops of his cheekbones. The eyes blinked a few times as the unusual request was considered, with the result that he produced a seemingly reluctant, "Aye."

"Can you get me there in ten minutes?" Tony tore at the door handle and flung himself into the back seat. "I have to make the plane going to Glasgow."

This took more consideration and, after a long pause, the driver said, "I make no promises," then shifted into gear.

It was not a long ride, which was a good thing since the cab was of venerable years and hurled itself down the road at a magnificent fifteen miles an hour; Tony would have preferred an engine overhaul to the cut-glass vase of flowers in the passenger compartment. In stately splendor they trundled out of Campbeltown and down a road through the fields that apparently led only to the Machrihanish Royal Air Force Base. This mystery was explained when, just before entering the base itself, the road turned off and skirted the end of the runway, following the signs to the British European Airways Terminal. Another turn in the road revealed a traffic light, just turning red, and the taxi slowed to a stop. The ten minutes must be up, the plane must be leaving by now! Tony banged on the glass divider, then scratched it open with his fingernails.

"Drive on—I must make that plane. There aren't any cars coming."

"Can't do that. Can't pass a red light. And no cars coming because this is no a road. It's for the plane to cross."

A grade crossing for planes; Scotland had not revealed all its secrets yet. But this meant the plane was leaving. "Leaving!" he cried aloud. "I've missed it."

"No, just coming in. A wee bit late today. This happens sometimes."

With this reassurance Tony relaxed, settling back into the cushions, hearing the roar of approaching engines, prepared to watch the leviathan of the airways taxi past, his transport of delight that would bear him to safety.

Louder the engines roared and there, no more than a dozen

feet from him, waddled by the most incredibly ugly aircraft he had ever seen.

It looked like a boxcar with wings. The sides were perfectly flat, tipping not the slightest nod to streamlining, the tricycle landing gear permanently fastened into place. A single wing fixed to the top of the boxcar had squared off ends, as did the vertical rudders of the double tail. With a futile attempt at decoration these were adorned with painted-on bits of the British flag. All of this incredible apparatus, which looked like something assembled from a breakfast cereal box, was powered by two tiny engines that industriously, and noisily, whirred the propellers. This apparition lumbered away and the light changed to green.

"What was . . . that?" Tony asked, hoarsely.

The driver, who had obviously been asked the question before, in the same tone of voice, nodded gloomily.

"It's called the Short Skyliner, but folks here call it by other names. Holds fifteen passengers, or twelve with luggage. There used to be a big beautiful Trident flew from here to Glasgow. Och! Took it off, the English did, and found this thing."

He pronounced the word *English* as though it were a curse word, and perhaps it was. Tony wondered if the driver could possibly be a member of the underground nationalists, then decided not to worry about it. They pulled up to the small wooden building of the terminal at the same time as the plane and he hurriedly paid the taxi fare then rushed to the ticket counter.

"You are in luck, sir," the charming counter attendant said, all green eyes, red hair, freckles and cheering smile. "Just one seat left. I hope you don't have any luggage?" Her smile faded to a slight frown. Forewarned, he told her no and waved the paper bag as his only possession. The smile returned, the ticket was issued and he joined the other passengers at the boarding door.

It was very much like traveling by winged stagecoach. The incoming passengers climbed out, hurriedly it seemed to him, clambering down the inside of the door, which, swung from ropes and hinged at the bottom, proved to have steps on its inside face. An attendant, strap of uniform cap under his chin to keep it from blowing away in the arctic wind that had sprung up suddenly, went to the flat rear of the plane, where a stagecoach would have a luggage boot, and slid open the door to the luggage boot. Then the boarding passengers were waved forward and Tony stepped out briskly with the others. After all, the thing had gotten here safely from Glasgow so, presumably, it could return there in the same manner.

He had been assigned a window seat; he wondered if it really would be a good idea to look out. Buckling in, he clutched his package to him. The ground attendant clambered by and passed a sheaf of papers to the pilot, clearly visible through an open curtain a few feet forward, and gave him the cheerful news as well that the boot was closed.

This was it, the moment of truth. The engines roared to hideous, vibrating life. The attendant left the plane and began to close the door—then opened it again. He had to shout over the sound:

"Is Mr. Duncan McMillan here?"

Tony's seat mate, a stern man in a stern black suit, turned to the question and, after some murmuring, left the plane. But he returned quickly and the door was closed behind him and he sat again next to Tony, who was looking out the window at the wildly whipping grass on the field.

It wasn't until they were taxiing out that Tony turned to look at his seat mate and saw that the stern Duncan McMillan had not returned after all.

Willy, the bespectacled man from the house in Carradale, was sitting there in his stead.

NINE

Tony would have leapt to his feet had he not been restrained by the seat belt. Instead he vibrated and thrashed in place, staring unbelievingly at the man, who only smiled in return. "Willy Fraser is my name, you'll recall we met once before." He nodded at the answering silence. "Anthony Hawkin is your name, I do believe. Look there, what a magnificent view, a perfect day for flying."

While his attention had been diverted the plane's engines had buzzed like insane bees and had pulled the craft bodily into the air. The slate rooftops and blue harbor of Campbeltown were slipping by under them as they clawed vigorously upward while ahead, over the channel, a craggy island came into view.

"Arran," Willy said, noticing Tony's attention. "A very mountainous place. There's the highest peak there, Goat Fell, almost three thousand feet. Much of Scotland is like that." He cleared his throat and quoted: " 'O, Caledonia! Stern and wild,' that's Sir Walter Scott of course. 'Land of brown heath and shaggy wood, Land of the mountain and the flood.' It's a fine country we have here, Mr. Hawkin, so I hope you'll no be doing anything to try to hurt it."

"Me? All I want to do with Scotland is to leave it. It wasn't my idea to visit Scotland—or England either for that matter."

"I'm sorry about that. Scotland's a bonny fair place when you get to know it. It will be my pleasure to tell you more of its history when we return."

"No fast talking, Fraser. I'm on my way to London and I'll bet planes fly there all the time from Glasgow."

"They do. But it is my unhappy duty to tell you that you won't be on any of them. There will be a car waiting for us and we'll drive back tonight."

"You can't make me!"

"Me! Och, no. I'm more of a talker than a doer. There'll be a few wee lads waiting for us. I just came along to tell you not to do anything foolish."

"That's nice of you." Tony looked out of the window that now revealed nothing except unbroken cloud. Rain beat against the glass. "I don't see what you want me for."

Willy chuckled dryly. "You *do* have a sense of humor. But I'm afraid your friend the colonel with the long name has told us everything. He has been most co-operative."

"Juarez-Sedoño?" Willy nodded. "Did he also tell you that he and his thugs kidnapped me and forced me to come to Scotland?"

"That's not *quite* the way he relates it. After all, we have plenty of witnesses who saw the two of you walking and drinking together in Carradale. We know now you were in on the plot from the beginning and you also knew how to dispose of the money . . ."

"He's lying! Or mad—or both."

"Is he? He said you were carrying part of the ransom money, and we know you cashed some of it today."

Tony's hand made an inadvertent movement toward his pocket, watched keenly by Willy. He jerked it away angrily. "That's not true. Or not the whole truth. I can explain everything."

"We hope you will, Mr. Hawkin, as soon as we get back."

"I won't go."

"It will be a shame if you do not change your mind. I don't like violence since I'm no a man of violence myself. But there are times when it is needed, the ends justify the means, and this appears to be one of the times."

"Oh no they don't." Tony clutched the seat arms as the plane fought its way through solid-seeming clouds. "There are no ends

—just means. And yours are pretty dirty—first skyjacking, then murder."

"I regret that as much as you do. It was all the doing of Angus Macpherson, who was an angry and violent man, God rest his soul. It was an unhappy accident when the Cuban died. But many have died for Scotland, and many more will do so in the future. Since 1746 we have been an occupied country, under control of a foreign power, the longest occupation of a country in the world's history. But now we're fighting back and neither you, nor anyone else, will stand in the way."

He was breathing heavily when he finished saying this, and his glasses were fogging up. He took them off—his eyes were amazingly mild in juxtaposition to the fierceness of his arguments—and polished them on his handkerchief. The pilot's voice rattled loudly through the loudspeaker:

"We have now reached our cruising altitude of thirteen thousand feet. Please see that your safety belts are fastened because we will be coming in for landing at Glasgow Airport."

Tony glanced at his watch. Wonderful, fifteen minutes to claw their way to this dizzy altitude—and now they were coming down to land. Patches of land were visible through the cloud, coming closer, and he wondered how to get out of this one. The Scots had the colonel—he hadn't been in the VW after all—and were obviously putting him to the question. The colonel was lying like a trooper and seeing that everyone was involved except himself. This co-operation was not healthy and Tony had no desire at all to be interrogated by their joint forces. Houses tilted up under the wing and they dropped sharply. A long runway swung into view and the plane hurled itself down toward it, bucking and pitching in the gusty wind. Tony knew his last moments had come. To die so far away from home!

With energetic countermovements the pilot fought the Skyliner across the sky, lifting a wing that tried to jam into the ground and forcing the careening machine to obey his will. A last effort sent them to the runway on a fairly level basis and the wheels touched. Braking and reversed propellers brought them to an immediate crawl and they taxied toward the terminal. It was raining again. Tony knew what he had to do. While those about him were involved in unbuckling their belts and all the bustle of leaving he pushed his wallet into the crack of the seat cushion.

A uniformed attendant opened the door and led his small flock across the rain-swept concrete to the arrival gate. Tony walked as slowly as possible, well aware of the hovering form of Willy by his side, and examined with close attention the physical setup of the airport. The terminal was off to the right, from which there projected an elevated and enclosed walkway. Stairs descended on both sides at regular intervals and they were going toward the nearest now, numbered seven. Presumably the gates were in the walkway above, and at the gate would be waiting Willy's muscular friends. So what he must do now was to avoid this gate and those unwelcome patriots.

By strolling, while the others rushed to be out of the scudding rain, Tony managed to be the last one through the door, climbing the stairs with the gateman right behind him. At the head of the stairs was a waiting room and ticket counter with other uniformed airline employees and a murmuring crowd beyond the barrier. This was far enough.

"Gone," Tony said, scratching at his hip and turning to the gateman. "My wallet is gone. It must have fallen out of my pocket in the plane."

"Are you sure, sir?"

"Positive. I had it out during the flight. Must not have put it away too securely. I'll go look." He turned back to the stairs and was aware of Willy vibrating back and forth by his side; Tony smiled affectionately. "No point in both of us getting wet, is there, Willy? You just wait here while I go get it."

The most senior of the uniformed employees had been listening to all this and nodded his permission. "Go with the gentleman, Donald, and see if you can find it."

Willy opened his mouth to protest—but there was really nothing he could say. He was the man of theory, not practice, and could not think fast enough. Tony waved to him thoughtfully and turned away back down the stairs. Step one.

"Does it always rain here?" he asked as they hurried back to the plane.

"Aye," Donald said, then thought about it. "That is when the sun is not shining." Mustn't frighten the tourists. "Do you remember which seat you were in?"

Tony pointed through the open door. "That one, front row on the right by the window." Donald climbed in, poked around the seat and retrieved the wallet. "Here it is, right as rain."

As they walked back to the exit Tony casually asked, "Are all these other gates exits as well?"

"Aye."

"Any particular reason why I could not use the next one down? It's closer to the terminal."

"Sorry. This is the exit for this flight."

"I would like to use the other one, no one should mind."

"Wrong exit, if you please."

A firm hand on the small of his back moved him politely but positively toward the waiting door. Tony opened his hands and the bag of clothing was caught by the wind and carried off in the direction of the North Pole. He grabbed for it but managed to miss. It rolled along the wet concrete, the paper disintegrating as he took a feeble step after it. His watchdog had better reflexes and ran ahead of him, reaching for the sack. They were under the walkway, out of sight of anyone above. Tony turned and ran toward the next exit.

He was only halfway there when angry shouts and pounding feet came after him. The soundproofing would keep anyone above from hearing this—so all he had to do was stay ahead of his pursuer. Fear winged his heels and he clawed the door open and pounded up the stairs. The counter above was vacant and he slowed to a fast walk as he went through the gate, very cheered to see the crowd at exit seven all had their backs turned to him.

Within the instant this changed. Irate and bellowing, his pur-

suer came through the door and all the heads snapped around
at once. Taking a deep breath, Tony plunged away down the
corridor. There were some passengers coming toward him and
he went through them with a neat bit of broken field running,
leaping nimble as a deer over a blockade of suitcases. He risked
a single look back over his shoulder as he pushed open the door
to the terminal.

The uniformed Donald had given up the chase, perhaps real-
izing that once inside the building Tony's crime became no
crime. Others felt differently. Two solidly built young men were
pounding along in his wake, trailed far behind by a panting
Willy. Press on!

Across the waiting room, quick glimpses of counters and shops,
a wide stairs ahead. Down it two steps at a time to collide with
a large dog on a leash. The dog blinked phlegmatically as Tony
fell, skidded, rolled and staggered to his feet. "Sorry," he said to
the dog's gaping owner as he thrust himself against the glass
doors to the sidewalk outside. Welcome as a lifesaver to a drown-
ing man was the waiting taxi. With his last strength he threw
himself inside and slammed the door behind him.

"To Glasgow," he gasped. "The Central Station." It was the
only place he knew.

The driver slowly started the engine and pushed it into gear
as the two pursuers rushed up. Tony fumbled with the door and
managed to press the locking button as they tore at the handle.

"My brother-in-law," he shouted with manic inspiration. "He
thinks I have not done right by his little sister."

The cab pulled slowly away, the driver nodding his head, some
common chord of humanity struck. "You should meet my bloody
in-laws," he said, grimly.

The scene through the rear window was most satisfying. The
two men ran a few feet, then stopped, shaking their fists after
the cab. They were joined by a staggering Willy and one of them
supported him while they conferred. The last glimpse Tony
had was of them waving down the next taxi in line. "They're
after us in a taxi," Tony said. "Is there anything you can do? I

have an extra five pounds here that might give you some ideas."
The cab shot forward as the driver stepped on the accelerator.

"In-laws," he said, voice rich with loathing, uniting all in-laws
in the world into a common band of evil. "I'll just turn here
where they can't see me and go right around and in the entrance
again. That way we'll be behind instead of ahead of them and
they won't have a clue."

It was a simple and masterful plan and Tony slowly regained
his breath as, at a safe distance, they followed the other cab from
the terminal. It shot ahead on the M8 motorway toward Glasgow
and they followed at a more leisurely pace until it finally left
them behind in the traffic. The driver, chuckling to himself with
the sweetness of some secret revenge, left the motorway before
they reached the city and they never saw the other taxi again.

As his fatigue faded so did Tony's elation. So he had given
them the slip. So what? He was still here in Scotland, plunging
toward a strange city with every man's hand turned against him.
A fugitive from the law, sought by Cuban torturers and Scotch
murderers, unshaven and tired. What to do? Go back to the airport and take a plane? No, that would mean facing the irate
Donald and the law, who would surely take a dim view of his
galloping flight through the terminal. Lie low in Glasgow in a
hotel or something? Unwise; that would just be putting off the
moment when he had to get out, permitting them to draw the
net tighter. He was moving now and he had to keep moving, stay
ahead if possible. The station it would have to be. Get a train
and get out.

Firm in his resolution, he tried to relax in his seat as they
worked their way through the early evening traffic. His stomach,
unstoked for a good twelve hours now, sent up frantic messages
that he was on the verge of starving to death. He beat it back
forcefully and ignored the siren attractions of all the restaurants
they passed. Flight first, eat later. The familiar bulk of Central
Station loomed ahead and he counted out pound notes, paid
handsomely even before the meter was turned off, bounding into
the station the instant they had stopped. There was a call board

that announced the trains and he was working it out to himself, take twelve away from all the numbers bigger than twelve and you have P.M., when a paunchy man stopped next to him, also examining the board.

"You would be much wiser to come with me, Mr. Hawkin," the man said in a low voice. Tony resisted strongly the impulse to leap straight into the air or to start running again. Instead he hurried toward the gate where the London train was boarding; it would not leave for another ten minutes. Of course they would have alerted lookouts at all the stations, not thugs but true believers. The thugs would be here soon.

"Ticket," the trainman at the gate said, raising his clipper and snapping it hopefully in Tony's direction.

"I can get it on the train." Hope raised, firmly dashed. "Ticket window there, sir. Next." He nipped little pieces from the slips of pasteboard as the passengers hurried past.

What to do? Numbly he stumbled off, feeling the forces of the enemy drawing close. As he passed a woman selling flowers from a basket she leaned forward and hissed around her solitary front tooth, "They're coomin' for you, Hawkin." It was too much! He rushed to the ticket window.

"Give me a ticket to London."

"Single or return?" He saw Tony's vacant expression so, no stranger to soft foreigners, he proceeded to translate. "One way or round trip?" A glance at Tony's unshaven jaw and clothes. "Second class." No question of that.

"One way, single, yes."

He paid, came away with the ticket in his hand, looked at the trains and had his first glimmer of hope. If he attempted to take the London train, he knew, without a doubt, that he would not be aboard it when it reached its destination. So what else? On the very next track stood a train, going to Edinburgh said the sign, leaving in one minute announced the clock. Whistles were already blowing on the platform, doors slamming, the trainman's hand ready on the entrance gate. A late arrival supplied the clue. He rushed up, brandishing his ticket—and was waved through. No time for the old clip-clip.

Don't all waved tickets look the same?

Walking with a slow rocking gait that he hoped radiated an aura of relaxation and ease, Tony strolled over toward the London train. Other passengers pushed past him since he was in no hurry; out of the corners of his eyes he watched the next gate with fierce intensity. More whistles blew and the trainman looked over his shoulder, then began to close the barrier.

"My train!" Tony called out, pushing through, ticket a-wave.

"Too late," the trainman said dourly, but allowed him to proceed. The train was beginning to move. He ran. Catching up with the last car, he wondered what to do next. How did the door open? He was beginning to tire and the train was going faster now.

The door popped open and a great black face looked down at him, an equally black hand took his and drew him forcefully in and the door slammed behind him. A whistle screamed as they gathered up speed and rushed out of the station.

"Thanks," Tony gasped at his savior.

"Nothing, mon, nothing."

He collapsed into the seat across from the man, who smiled benevolently upon him. His coat was shabby and his shoes were scuffed; a crumpled paper bundle rested comfortably in his lap. A generous smile lit his face, stretching his face below his wide broken nose, wide to begin with and now covering a good part of the center of his face. With conspiratory discretion he looked around to be sure the compartment was empty, it was, then produced with a display of pride a long-necked amber bottle from his package.

"True Jamaica rum, straight from home. You drink that and you'll be feeling better."

"I would," Tony gasped and took the bottle and drank deep; it seared a track of joy down his parched gullet. His newfound companion nodded compassionately and had a deep draught himself, smacking his lips with relish afterward. There was a rattle of the compartment door as the conductor slid it open and the bottle instantly vanished.

"Tickets."

The clipper snicked once, then he turned to Tony and took the proffered ticket and looked at it appraisingly.

"This is a ticket for London and you're on the Edinburgh train."

"I must have made a mistake."

"No good on this train, but you can change in Edinburgh. But you'll need a ticket to get there."

"I can buy one can't I?"

The answer was obviously yes for the conductor produced forms and tickets from his pockets and did laborious calculations, accepting money and returning a receipt. Tony pocketed this, paid the required sum and watched the door close with relief.

"I can tell that you are American," his traveling companion said. "And that is my part of the world too, we drink to that." They did. "Teddy Buchanan," he added, smiling, like a benediction.

"What? Oh, yes, I'm . . . George Wash." He managed to swallow the *ington*. Yes, that was American enough; what could he have been thinking of?

"Pleased to make your acquaintance, George. I like to talk, have a drink with a mon, makes the trip much faster. People here aren't like in Jamaica, don't like to do that. Here."

Here was another slug of liquid fire. Tony's head was beginning to buzz with the impact of the decidedly raw spirits on his empty stomach. Food would take care of that, yes food, long forgotten. Was there anything to eat on this train? Teddy nodded at the question.

"A nice buffet car, come I'll show you. Every Saturday I make this trip, see my friend's wife, who is in hospital in Glasgow. I talk to her, cheer her up, sometimes give her a little rum when sister is out of the way. It's a good life if you keep happy, isn't it?"

Tony nodded and fought back a hiccup as they trod the corri-

dor. Life certainly was happier when beamed upon by that smiling face; he felt better already. Edinburgh was hovering in the
future and he would arrive there soon enough. But that problem
would be faced when it arrived, along with the problem of the
unwelcome welcoming committee that he had no doubt would be
waiting for him in the station. Food first and problems later! In
this he was in luck for the buffet car proved to be a highly civilized arrangement, with tables between the facing seats and a
sort of compact ship's galley in the center where good things of
all kinds were dispersed. Coffee and freshly brewed tea, packages of cakes and pies, sandwiches and potato chips. Ranked
rows of strong drink, an infinite variety of alcoholic and teetotal
beverages in cans. "Sandwiches?" Tony asked hopefully.

"Cheese and tomato, egg and cress, ham, salmon."

"Yes."

"Pardon?"

"One of each. And the same for my friend here." He cut off
a protestation with a raised hand. "A man can't eat alone. And
some beer."

Their arms filled, they found an empty table, where they went
promptly to work. Teddy, as solid a trencherman as the starving
Tony, ate his supplies with great gusto. It all disappeared very
quickly and Tony went for some whisky to hold it down. This
was dispensed in tiny bottles, so he bought a number of them
to keep from running back and forth.

"You have a warm heart," Teddy announced, "so we drink to
that. Too bad we will be in Edinburgh soon and end such a good
party."

Edinburgh! Tony had put it from his mind for the pleasures
of the moment; his spirits and his face fell. What to do? "Do
you know the city well?"

"Been there almost two years now. Winters are terribly long.
But spring looks better that way."

"The station where we get in—is it big? I mean if someone
were to not want to meet someone else in that station is there
a different way out or something like that?"

"I knew the moment I first saw you you were getting away from the police."

"No, really . . ."

Teddy touched a large, silencing finger to his lips and made shushing noises. "My momma always told me what the eye does not see the heart does not grieve. I imagine the same is true for what the ear do not hear. The rozzers will be waiting for you?"

"No, not the police, I guarantee you that. Just some people I don't want to meet."

Teddy drank a small bottle of whisky straight in order to lubricate his thoughts, screwing up his face and looking skyward for inspiration. "No back way. Everyone has to pass the barrier to turn in tickets. I suppose your friends will be waiting there. Lots of ways out then, but no way to stop from being followed. You could take a cab?"

"They could follow me."

"Bad idea cabs, expensive too." The whisky was promoting no new thoughts so he surreptitiously tipped some rum into his glass, warm homely stimulation from a happier clime. "Now that's it, that is the very idea. There is a hotel right on top of the station, the North British Hotel, and just opposite the trains is a hall that leads to a private lift that goes up to that hotel. A long quiet hall that turns a corner. You just take that lift up to the hotel and walk out onto Prince's Street and be on your way. By the time they come the long way around you will be well gone."

"But what is to stop them from coming up with me in the elevator?"

"Me." Teddy smiled warmly and closed a dark fist about the size of a soup bowl. "I am a man of peace but do not like to see my friends molested."

"I can't ask you to do that."

"You did not ask, I suggested as you will recall. Will there be more than five of them?"

"I doubt it, one or maybe two in the most, but . . ."

"Why that will be fun. No need to fight, then. Just talk to them in a jolly manner for a bit until the lift leaves."

Tony protested to no avail. In Teddy's world a friend was a friend, new or old, and what else were friends for if not to help one another? He frowned only when Tony mentioned money.

"Now, George, why do you want to go and talk like that?"

"No, not for you . . . I was thinking of . . . your friend's wife," Tony improvised hurriedly; Teddy's smile returned instantly. "If you are going to help me, why can't I help her? If you give her ten, twenty pounds from me I'll bet there are plenty things she could spend that on."

"You are so right. My friend only works part time in the shipyard, hard to make do with that. She will appreciate it." The bills vanished and they drank to friendship. Outside, the dark landscape raced by, broken here and there by the lights of a lonely house, a car on a road. Soon the houses gathered together, streetlights appeared, the suburbs of a large city sprang up. The train rattled across switches and slowed, swaying from side to side.

"Coming into Waverly Station now," Teddy announced, finishing the last of the little bottles. "You must see me again if ever you get back to Edinburgh—let me give you my address." He wrote it, slowly and carefully, on one of the napkins, which Tony pocketed. "Let us take our time. Anyone else using the hotel lift will be arriving in first class, and we want them to clear away."

They were among the last of the passengers to leave, surrendering their tickets as Tony searched the crowd. Was it possible there would be no welcoming committee? It was not possible. As they crossed the station away from the main body of passengers, three men, dressed alike in trench coats, sauntered after them. "Your friends?" Teddy asked, jerking a thumb cheerfully in their direction. Tony nodded. "No problem at all—this will be good fun."

The sturdy Jamaican had a far different idea of fun than Tony had. They entered a passageway brightly decorated with railroad murals on the wall, with a turn at the far end.

"Right," Teddy announced, taking Tony's hand. "It was good

meeting you, that is a long dull train trip otherwise." He squeezed lightly, numbing Tony's fingers, patted him on his back to send him on his way, then carefully deposited his precious package against the wall, safe from harm, before turning to face their pursuers. "Run," he said, and Tony did. His last view as he turned the corner was of the solid figure, fists on hips and legs widespread, standing in the path of the rushing men.

Of course the elevator was not there, though a silver-haired woman, with just a touch of blue at the ends of her hair and nose, was waiting before the closed door. From around the corner loud voices were raised in protest, countered by a soft but firm reply. She looked frightened and jabbed at the button. Tony whistled and admired a mural, aware of nothing. There was the scuffle of shoes and a sharp, plocking sound. Indelicate language was spoken. The elevator doors opened and the woman hurried in, Tony at her heels. They both stabbed at the button marked LOBBY; there was a roar of pain fading quickly into the distance as the doors closed. They rose slowly, in silence and solitude. Teddy had been as good as his word. But what next?

Move fast, whatever he did he had to do fast. Up until now he had had no idea of escape other than getting out of the hotel and mingling with the Saturday night crowds. No crowds in the lobby, however. Warm wood panels, rugs underfoot, a string quartet playing somewhere close-by. His elevator companion turned left so Tony turned right toward a vision of distant revolving doors. Stay ahead of them. Down the corridor past the barbershop, still open, business slow, the barber himself standing by the door looking hopefully at the passers-by. Tony slowed, looked in, thought. The barber, little business for his own business with a shiny bald head, took the hesitation for a greater interest and pointed inward temptingly.

"You're next, sir." As though Tony were first in an interminable cue stretching to the horizon. Was it possible?

"I need a shave?"

"Very good, sir."

Why not! He folded his raincoat and cap out of sight on a chair, despite the barber's attempts to hang them up, then hurried to the chair. Feet high, striped cloth draped, tense moments before the lather was applied. After this, relief unfettered. He actually had the sharp pleasure of seeing, when the barber stepped aside to strop his razor, one of the burly trio from the station hurry by in the corridor outside. He had his hand to his jaw as he went and walked with a definite limp, sparing the barbershop only a brief glance as he passed. Done!

To the barber's delight, Tony partook of all the establishment offered; mud pack to soothe his razor-rasped face, haircut, singe, scalp massage with vibrator. It all took quite a while. The barber caught the spirit of Tony's dalliance and, after trimming his eyebrows and clipping a few hairs from his nose, could only step back and sigh, resources drained. A brushing was all that was left, he made the most of that, and accepted his payment as just due.

Nor had Tony wasted his time in the chair. He had pondered and rejected a number of plans until he found one that seemed most satisfactory. Since the barbershop ruse had worked so well, any pursuit must have fanned out from this center. It might be wise to remain just where he was, in the hotel above. An overwhelming fatigue added credence to the suggestion. With his new clothes and tonsorial splendor he looked neat enough for the role. Slip upstairs under a false name, lie low until the morrow—then think about getting to London. A safe den for the moment was not to be despised. It would do fine.

A young and seemingly bored clerk nodded with fatigue at his request for a room.

"Do you have a reservation, sir?"

"No, plans changed, stay overnight, you know . . ."

"I think we can accommodate you. Single with bath, for one night. Will you fill out the form, please?"

Success. Pen poised, Tony wondered what would be an improvement over old George Wash for the register when the clerk's voice penetrated his concentration.

"If I could have your passport . . ."

TEN

"Passport, passport?" A cracked recording of a parrot voice.

"Yes, sir. You will see the space for the passport number here in the registration form. It is a law that all foreigners must register their passport numbers."

Memories of an Empire widespread, a Commonwealth contracting, surged wildly through Tony's mind. "But I'm not a foreigner. Not really. Canadian." Scenes from a war movie seen recently on television shot by. "You weren't asking our chaps for passports when we were here after the Dieppe raid." He began filling out the form furiously. French Canadian, that's what, subtle touch there. *Jean Auguste Dominique Ingres,* name memorized for an art history exam long since dust, his own Washington address for want of better inspiration, *Quebec, Canada.* Had he spelled Quebec right? Too late now to worry; he pushed the form back across the desk with a flourish.

A key appeared, victory was his, the Dieppe raid successful after all the years. "That will be ten pounds, twenty-five with breakfast. Do you have any luggage, Mr. Ing-riss?"

"No. So I imagine you wouldn't mind if I paid in advance?"

No protests were made. An octogenarian bellhop appeared to clutch the key and shuffle a course to the left. At the room he unlocked the door, turned on the lights, opened the window, closed the curtains and did all the other traditional things bellhops do to remind guests of their tip-prone presence. Tony produced coins.

"Do you know if there are any trains to London tomorrow morning?"

"Head porter has the schedule."

"I'm a little too tired to see the head porter, in fact I'm very tired. If I gave you some money do you think you could find out when there is a train, buy me a ticket and bring it to me in the morning?" Bills rustled. "This one is for you." Why had he ordered a ticket when he already had one? He must be tired.

"First class, of course, sir? Single?"

"Of course. Of course."

Escape provided for, fatigue leapt instantly upon him. Within a minute the bed was embracing him with feathery arms and oblivion descended. The next thing he was aware of was a discreet knocking that dredged him from the depths of slumber, blinking and trying to remember where he was and what he was doing here. A key rattled and the ancient bellhop shuffled in with a tray. A tug on the cord sent actinic sunlight searing into Tony's eyes and by the time his vision had cleared there was a cup of tea on the bedside table, with an envelope beside it.

"It's the ten-fourteen, sir, a fine train. Plenty of time for breakfast before you leave."

The tea, stronger, hotter and a lot better than any he had ever had before, started the blood moving sluggishly through his veins and he went to shower to wake up. This proved impossible, room with bath meant just that, so he settled for a long soak, which, in many ways, was far superior. Baths, from Archimedes onward, have ever been the site of thought and he had a good deal of thinking to do.

Item: the Scotch liberationists were still on his trail and would surely be watching all the trains. He should be able to board his easily enough—but how to get off in safety? As long as they believed he was involved in the disappearance of the skyjack money they would be after him.

Item: the police would certainly be looking for him by now after the cashing of the marked bills. They were to be avoided as much as the Scotchmen.

Item: if he was ever to extricate himself from this mess he had to find the money and the man who had stolen it from the house in Carradale. He had some thoughts and suspicions on that subject but in order to do anything about them he needed help.

Item: the only help freely given so far in these British Isles had been by the jovial Teddy Buchanan—may he prosper forever!—and another visitor from the warmer parts of the world.

A quick scratch through his wallet produced the card and, after a little linguistic difficulty with the operator, a phone could be heard ringing miles away in distant London.

"Cohn's Fancy Bakery."

"Onion bagel."

"Nu, onion bagel? So what with onion bagel?"

"Listen, I was told to call this number and say onion bagel and then something would happen."

"Sure something's going to happen, I'm going to tell you to drop dead. . . ." There was the sound of angry voices and the receiver rattled loudly against something, then a different man's voice spoke:

"Hello. What did you say?"

"Onion bagel, that's all, just onion bagel!"

"Right. Sorry about that—we have a new baker. Is this Hawkin?"

"Yes, of course. Is Esther there?"

"No, but she said if you called we were to help you. What's up?"

"Me, up in Scotland. But I'm coming back to London on the ten-fourteen train out of Edinburgh this morning. I don't know what time or where it arrives but I imagine that is the sort of thing that can be found out easily enough. My problem is that there will either be people on the train with me or some waiting in London who will want me to go away with them. I don't want to go with them. Is there anything . . . ?"

"No problem, Mr. Hawkin, no problem at all. This is the kind of service we are happy to provide. I'll see you at the station."

That was taken care of. With the immediate future provided for, rested and cleansed, his appetite pounced. He pulled his sweater on over his shirt, it would have to do since his jacket was still at the Glasgow airport. But no eyes were raised in sartorial protest when he entered the breakfast room, wood-paneled and well-lit, lights twinkling from the battery of silverware at each place, the soothing white of the tablecloths. He ordered with vicious attention, first orange juice to let his stomach know that more was coming, then porridge—no more oatmeal, he was learning fast—to establish a foundation. After this something advertised as egg, bacon and tomato that turned out to be a deliciously grilled tomato, meaty bacon, an egg cooked in hot fat, toast from a special metal rack designed to take all the heat from it, some orange marmalade for the rest of the toast, all washed down by a pot of tea. Life, internally at least, had never looked better. All this was timed nicely to match the train. With minutes to go he checked out, bought some newspapers and magazines from the stand in the lobby—then finally descended to the station at the last possible moment. Looking neither right nor left, he hurried to the platform and had just found his compartment when the train began moving. There were white doilies on the seats, which also seemed to be a bit wider and covered with a superior grade of prickly velvet than second class. The only other occupant was a thin man in army uniform with a clerical collar who was reading the *Church Times,* and who seemed completely unaware of Tony's presence, even when he trod, with apologies, on his toes when he entered. Rum and smiles were from a different part of the world. A change of scene was certainly called for and he elicited information from the conductor when he presented his ticket.

"Buffet coach at Carlisle in one hour, when we join the Glasgow train." A British Rail map on the wall explained this circumstance. Apparently trains left from Glasgow and Edinburgh at the same time, then joined up in Carlisle and became a single train for the rest of the journey south. Fate, or Scotch eating and drinking habits, had ruled that the buffet car would be on the Glasgow section. Forcefully deprived of drink, he found himself a prisoner of a raging thirst, made worse by thoughts of eternity prompted by the silent padre. He sought to distract himself with reading, but the headlines only reminded him of his predicament. There was some small pleasure to be derived from sharing his troubles with none less than the U. S. Government. It seemed that all of the Arab countries had honored their promises and had forked over the ransom money—with a single exception. The country was not named, but dark hints were dropped that they would be declaimed before the world if they didn't ante up the promised $200,000. Very interesting. The rest of the news was about strikes, inflation, rising food prices —he might have been reading a newspaper at home for all the difference it made. The magazines did not interest him, not with the thought of a large whisky interfering with his concentration, so he threw them aside and walked the corridor, counting the minutes and wondering, not for the first time, what he was doing in this fix.

Carlisle eventually hauled itself slowly over the horizon and they rattled into the yards. There was much backing and stopping until the two sections were joined and coupled. Tony was hovering at the door when it was unlocked and was the first through. The buffet car was doing a roaring business—they had had an hour advantage of him—and he attempted quickly to catch up. For reasons best known to British Rail, larger bottles of Scotch whisky were available on this train and he obtained one, along with a glass, a tiny shred of ice and a can of warm soda water. Cigars were available as well so he bought a Dutch panetella and indulged himself. It was all very satisfying until he noticed the landscape was moving again outside—but directly opposite from the way it had been moving earlier.

"We're going in the wrong direction!" he said aloud.

"Och, aye, south," the man behind the bar answered, gloomily polishing a glass, and the customers all nodded in agreement. Scots nationalism was a power to be reckoned with, he realized. Someone kindly explained that the coaches were turned around in the shunting yard and they were indeed going to London, not back to Scotland. After this he was part of the conversation and heard much arcane lore about the sport of football and in exchange answered a number of questions about America. Hunger tweaked a bit after twelve, but fresh sandwiches took care of that. All too soon they were pulling into London and he had to hurry back to his compartment to retrieve his raincoat and cap. The military clerical must have found some deep truth in his newspaper because he had spread it over his face and was snoring heavily behind it. Tony crept out and was one of the first to disembark in the cavernous station. A now, unhappily, familiar band of grim Highland faces faced him, four men in all, all strangers but all alike in their steadfast determination. A large red hand seized his arm, clutching it firmly.

"If you no give us trouble, we'll no give you trouble. There's a car ootside and we're getting into it."

"Tony—how wonderful to see you here," a gentler voice called out. Esther Ben-Alter strolled up, bewitching in a bright red, tightly cinched raincoat, and kissed him on the cheek. His four would-be captors formed behind him, unsure but steadfast. Esther looked pointedly at each of them.

"It would be best if you let go of this gentleman and left quietly. The two nice young men who are standing next to you really are specialists in the martial arts and sincerely don't want to harm you . . ."

"Move aside—we're armed."

"Well we're not and it makes no difference."

It didn't. The speaker attempted to pull a gun from his pocket as he turned but there was a swift motion and he stopped turning and slid slowly down until a companion clutched his unconscious form and supported it. The other two also tried to protest but there were more quick moves, most of which Tony did not see, and very quickly they were all seated on a baggage truck, two with their eyes closed, the other two barely conscious.

"I'm glad to see you," Tony said.

"The feeling is a mutual one," she assured him. "I have a number of interesting things to tell you and hope you have things to tell me as well. Meanwhile, meet my associates, Jinon and Isaj."

Tony shook two hard brown hands as they walked. "Jacob Goldstein told us you were a good friend of his," one of them said. Which was it? They were very much like twins. "He said we were to help you whenever we could."

"Tell Jake thanks when you see him and your help is much appreciated."

They took a cab from the rank in front of the station, the two muscular sabers sitting on the facing jump seats, arms folded and silent, matched interior outriders. No one seemed interested in talking in the cab so the ride proceeded with silence on all sides. Tony admired the double-decked red buses and the hurrying traffic, shop fronts and parks. Their vehicular destination proved to be a street corner in a rugged-looking section of the city. Their final destination was a good three blocks farther on. Eternal vigilance is the life of the secret agent. Nor was their path that direct. First they went down stairs set in the sidewalk where a sign promised entrance to a subway. No trains were in evidence, simply a tunnel under the street. Very mysterious. What would a real subway be called? Probably an "underground" or something like that. After this there were narrow passages between buildings, an entrance to an office building with an exit on a different street and, finally, their destination. This proved to be a dark, peeling building with a large sign over the entrance that read The Marmion, with the smaller message below that it offered Bed & Breakfast. All of the windows were shut tight and badly in need of washing, while a general seedy air of decay radiated from every stone. Tony looked at it suspiciously; Esther caught the glance.

"It's not much to look at, which is far from accidental. Some of the accommodations are really quite comfortable. There are plenty of people going in and out all the time, which makes it a good cover. We can get you a room here, if you want, that is if you are worried about the skyjackers still being after you." Tony cocked his head dubiously. "Gefilte fish for breakfast," she added, seeing his hesitation, further temptation to convince him to make up his mind.

"I think it is just what I need, thank you for offering, and I would love to stay here. But there is something I must do first." He noticed her raised eyebrows. "No, really, there are some things I have to find out and they might be dangerous. A phone call, that's all. I'll make it someplace away from here and will then be right back. You have my word."

She smiled and patted his arm. "Whatever you say, the door is always open."

Tony made a note that the lodging house was on Lamb Street, easy enough to remember, as being led to the slaughter—what had made him think of that connection!—and he went briskly around the corner and away until he saw a roving cab.

"Piccadilly Circus," he told the driver. It was the only place in London he knew, other than Scotland Yard; no thank you! He must get a map, learn his way around. Learn where the centers of cultural interest were, see the paintings in the National Portrait Gallery, the Tate . . . his thoughts spiraled downward into gloom. What was he thinking about? Every man's hand, with the exception of a few Jewish ones, was turned against him. And he was wanted by the police, or maybe he was not wanted by the police. That was what he had to determine now, the reason why he had slipped away from his Israeli saviors. He had to find out what Scotland Yard's position was on the hot money that he had passed. A phone call to the United States Embassy was in order to determine just what his status was.

Eros danced lightly before him in the Circus as he paid off his driver. Scotland Yard was down that way and over there the hotel where he was known, so he quickly turned his back and walked away from them both. This led him across a narrow street filled with rushing cabs to a doorway where a man in a white apron was unlocking and opening a metal grille. As he did this a glass sign above the door flashed to life, green letters against white, spelling out O'Flaherty's Irish House. The doorway and the simple sign were like nothing he had ever seen before, but somehow they plucked an alcoholic string within him. It had been some time, an hour at least, since he had had any beverage and his system was sending out little whimpering messages for restoking of the internal flames.

"Are drinks served here?" he asked the aproned man who had secured the open grille into place.

"Sure and if the're not oive been in the wrong business for many years."

Thus reassured, and following two other men hurriedly bent on the same errand, he treaded the steep stairs down into an underground specie of saloon quaintly walled with New York subway toilet tiles, cracked and aged in places but still well polished. Like an island in a sea of thirst, an oval mahogany bar stood in the center of the room, with racked glasses and bottles pendant above, beer-pump handles projecting from below. "Half of Guinness," the first arrival said to a red-cheeked bartender who looked all of fourteen years old. This lad turned away instantly, began pulling on a wood and brass handle, and his place was taken by another barkeep of the same age and complexion. "Half of Guinness and a Paddy's," the second man said. A dark mug of liquid appeared before each of them, along with a single glass of golden liquor. Always ready to learn, and not wanting to be outdone, Tony ordered a pint of Guinness to go with his Paddy.

It was a wise choice. Paddy proved, as well it might, to be a mellow Irish whiskey that blended serenely with the midnight soothing of the dark beverage, rich indeed, a meal in itself, but what could it be?

"Guinness?" the man next to him at the bar answered in response to his request for information. "Ahh, Guinness." He looked ceilingward as though for inspiration, a small man in a dusty derby, a number of days past his last shave, wearing a shirt without a collar like the ones in the old haberdasher shop ads. A relic of his youth—or was it possible that shirts without collars were still made in some parts of the world? "Yes, Guinness," he said looking back at Tony, some higher instruction received. "Why sure and 'tis the finest drink on God's green earth, brewed by the banks of the Liffey, though not from the water these days,

His Mercy save us, that water being the color of death itself. A stout, yes, a member of the beer family yet rising above their mundane pastures as a great tree rises up from a field of nettles. Mother's milk I have heard it referred to as many times, have ordered it myself that way, for it is maternal nourishment indeed. A jar of Guinness, or a glass as it is called in this part of the world, is medicine for the soul and liver such as no doctor need prescribe. When taken with a dram of whiskey, why it reaches heights of pleasure of a rarefaction more known to the angels than to mankind. That, your honor, is Guinness." He lowered his eyes over his glass reverently.

"Why, yes, thanks, I had no idea . . ."

"I must add that with a dram, as you are doing, it works wonders internally, as well as to the soul of the drinker. Being a poor man, unlike yourself, I rarely, if ever, indulge myself in that combination . . ."

The words faded into silence and fell to the bar between them and lay there curled up dustily as though waiting for a wet answer.

"Well, join me in one, won't you?"

"A pleasure." His glass rapped commandingly on the wood. "Patrick my boy, a large Paddy's for us both, and one for yourself since you have a thirsty look. And there's a hole in me jar, and in me friend's here, and he insists that they be filled."

They were, quickly enough, the youthful bartender murmuring his thanks and draining his glass, accepting Tony's money with alacrity. Tony's change was wet, pools of beer were rapidly forming on the bar, the bills sodden.

"Sure and there are other things about Guinness you should be knowing. 'Tis a noble adjunct to food, making any meal a repast, but is particularly known for its compatibility with the denizens of the sea, and of all these creatures the oyster in particular—look there and you will see what I mean." There was a tiled alcove occupied by a small bar laden with tubs of oysters. A number of these were being opened rapidly and professionally by a third teen-age bartender. Without conscious effort

Tony found himself and his newfound companion at this bar, glasses firmly in hand, looking down at two plates of these same oysters. Tony paid. The combination was indeed delicious and he made no protest when another dozen appeared. It was one way of getting rid of the soggy bills.

Halfway through another pint of Guinness, memory of his mission surfaced through the brown waves.

"Is there a telephone here?"

"Telephone, there is that. Through the door right next to the bog, you can't miss it, just follow your nose."

After much rattling through the numerous volumes of the London phone directory Tony found the embassy's number. There was a long list of instructions to be followed in order to make a call from a pay phone and he read them carefully, blinking often to clear away a sort of Guinness-colored fog that interfered with his vision. The call could be dialed without depositing money, in fact there were dire warnings and metal bars to prevent this. A certain button had to be pressed, dial, money, button —he finally mastered it after a couple of false tries and obtained a listening voice that assured him that this was the American Embassy, which was also closed.

"But I must contact . . ." Who should he contact?

"If you will leave your name I will see what I can do. . . . Hawkin . . . *Anthony* Hawkin? Yes, I have an extension here in case you should call. Please hold the line and I will connect you."

After rattles and mechanical mutterings a familiar voice came on the line. *"Is that you, Hawkin?"*

"Yes, but is that . . . ?" A gush of nostalgic memory. "It can't be, is that Ross Sones?"

"Of course."

"But you're in Washington."

"No I'm not. I'm here handling liaison over the money. Which is just what I want to talk to you about . . ."

"Scotland Yard is after me, that's what you were going to say."

"We have a bad connection, Hawkin. Get over here at once."

"The police want me, why don't you say so?"

"Hawkin, what's the trouble? I want to talk to you about you know what. Not on a public phone. The police aren't involved in any way."

"Sure, that's what you say, Sones." To Tony's ears the FBI man's voice dripped with insincerity. Well there was one easy way to find out.

"Look, Sones, I can't talk right now. I'm in a sort of restaurant and my food has just arrived. I haven't eaten in two days, I have to eat, I'm out of change for the phone. Look—here is the number of this phone. Call me back in twenty minutes, I'll be right here, and tell me what you want me to do. Good-bye."

Right here indeed! Shoving the sodden coins and bills deep into his pocket, he exited at a fast walk, waved farewell to his new friends and climbed the stairs to the street above. Not twenty yards away was an establishment whose windows had an enchanting selection of cardboard Buckingham Palaces, toy guardsmen, ash trays with Tower Bridge on them and other gimcrack dear to the heart of the tourist. By standing in the entrance between the two show windows he could pretend to admire these dubious objects while, at the same time, really looking through the windows and, unobserved himself, watch the entrance to the Irish House.

Many went down, none emerged, as though entering the underworld itself, and in less than five minutes his patience—and suspicions—were well rewarded.

Two policemen, official and stern in tall helmets and brass buttons, appeared and tramped through the doorway and down and out of sight.

ELEVEN

Remembering the precautions that the Israelis had taken, Tony attempted the same. A cab dropped him off some blocks distant from The Marmion and he skulked the rest of the way. One of the agents, Jinon or Isaj, sat on the steps drinking Paris green-colored soda pop from a bottle and did not look up when Tony passed. Yet he must have transmitted some signal for Esther came to meet him in the darkness of the hall.

"Is there any place we can talk quietly?" he asked.

"In the breakfast room, we won't be disturbed there. Would you like a bite to eat? A drink?"

"No, yes. I mean no, no. Unless you have coffee or tea or something like that." Memories of Guinness and Paddy's still cast a numbing miasma over his frontal lobes; he must cut down on the drink.

"A nice glass of tea. I'll be right back."

There was a single long table stretching the length of the room, already set with silverware for breakfast, jars of jam, salt and pepper. A hulking dark piece of furniture rested against one wall, bristling with drawers and knobs, its top bearing magazines and old newspapers while above this a portrait, all cigar and bulldogish scowl, of Churchill brightened the scene. Esther brought the tea and they sat at the far end of the table by the window. The upright spoon in the glass almost got him in the eye but he managed to duck under it to slurp the reviving beverage, washing the dark remains of Guinness from his throat.

"I'm in a little bit of trouble," he said offhandedly.

"Is that what they call American understatement? When I first met you there was an Al Fatah thug in your room trying to beat you up. Now you return to London to be met by a squad of Scots musclemen. Enough there to give anyone nightmares."

"Yes, but that's only the half of it. I was spirited away from London at gunpoint by a team of Cuban skyjackers who were in league with the Scotch nationalists and they fixed it to look as though I had cashed some of the marked skyjack bills and later I really did cash some so that, it looks, well . . ."

"Are the police after you too?"

He nodded unhappily. "Yes—but you won't turn me in, will you?"

"Never! As a spy myself I am a little outside the law. Not only that but Jacob would kill me if I allowed one hair of your head to be harmed. This is quite a track record you have accumulated after only a couple of days in the country. How are you getting along with the Pakistani Secret Service?"

"What do you mean? This is no joke . . ."

"I'm sorry, I never intended, here have more tea. I was only asking. They are very interested in the skyjacking as well since it looks like the weapons the gang used were loaded aboard in Karachi. I thought maybe they were onto you too."

"Well I've managed to miss them so far, thanks a lot."

"I'm sorry," she said soothingly. "I was just asking. Could your Cuban troubles have anything to do with Colonel Juarez-Sedoño?"

"You bet they do, he's the joker in charge of their whole operation. How much do you know?"

"A little that I will be happy to tell you. But first, please, tell me what has happened to you since I left you at the hotel."

Tony told, happy to gain tongue-clucking sympathy for the plight the colonel had put him in. Mile by mile he traced his adventures to Glasgow and thence to Carradale and Campbeltown. Esther refilled his tea glass as he flew to Glasgow and, seeing he needed something stronger to get him to Edinburgh, found a bottle of whisky to sustain him for the rest of the voyage. Old Mortality, a very sustaining scotch indeed, and it enabled him to survive the trip back to London and their meeting at the station.

"You *have* been busy," she said with professional approval. "Of course you were forced to change those hundred dollar bills to escape, but that will have to be proven later to the police. There is no point in giving yourself up until you are a bit closer to the truth."

"I'll agree to that. Now tell me what you know about the colonel."

"Not very much. We first learned of his existence when we followed an Al Fatah agent to his home. He has had dealings with them on and off for years, possibly trading in munitions. In any case he is in our books as a 'perhaps unfriendly.' And we did uncover the fact that he is in with the anti-Castro groups in England. So, as soon as we heard that Cubans were involved in the skyjacking, we put a watch on his house. I'm sorry we weren't quick enough to be there when they took you away, but we have had the place under observation ever since. In doing this we know we are one step ahead of the police, who have not yet linked the colonel with the skyjacking. There is one bit of intelligence that I know will be of interest to you. The colonel has a visitor, a young lady, who arrived yesterday and is still there. We don't know if she is remaining voluntarily, but she surely came there on her own. An Egyptian girl named Jasmin Sotiraki."

"The hostess from the plane!"

"The very one. The web of intrigue is getting very tangled but, to continue the simile, all of the strands seem to be leading in one direction."

"Well if you can make sense out of this whole thing I wish you would tell me. What has Jasmin got to do with the others?"

"She has long been an Al Fatah sympathizer so we are forced to conclude that they are involved in this affair as well. After all, you had one of their agents in your hotel room."

"You mean it might be an Al Fatah-Scotch-Cuban plot?"

"It looks that way. Stranger things have happened."

"Oh no they haven't! This one takes the record for confusion if nothing else. If you will permit me to count on my fingers in my slow Indian, art historian way—"

"Have some more scotch first."

"Why not. It can't make things any more obscure. All right. We have a great big DC-10 that is owned by a lot of Arabs, some of which are the Al Fatah. Somewhere along the line the Al Fatah gets involved with the Scotch Home Rule people who contact the Cuban counterrevolutionaries. They cook up a plan to skyjack the plane and it works. But something goes wrong when the Scotch decide they want all the money for themselves and grab it. So all of the others, along with the police, are after the Scotch, who, before they have time to do anything constructive to cast off the English yoke, are hijacked in return, their leader Angus Macpherson polished off in the robbery, and the money vanishes a second time. Which is where we are now, correct?"

"Correct—but with one single important addition. In the house in Carradale you heard the man, Willy, say that someone was in with Angus just before he was shot. Do you remember his exact words?"

"Not really, something about a fencing-cully."

"You have a fine memory. That is a slang term for a fence or receiver of stolen goods."

"Then it could be the fence who knocked off Angus in order to get the hot bills without paying for them?"

"It certainly looks that way. Which gives us a strong lead. Your pursuer Willy may know who this fence is. We must try to question him."

"Wait! Not only him, let me think." He took a deep drink from his glass without thinking, choked and began coughing on the strong spirits. Esther came around the table and pounded on his back and pounded the cough away and, apparently, memory back in. "The bundle of bills I took from the colonel was brought to him by Ramon from the plane. And I heard him say that they were for the fence. Samples to set the deal up I guess. Could it be the same fence?"

"Perhaps, perhaps not. But it is a lead and perhaps the only lead we have."

"Right—so we follow it up. If we can find the fence the Cubans planned to use he may be the murderer and the man with the money. If he is not he might very well know who the other fences are who could handle a deal like this."

"There is a very strong possibility that you may be correct. But is there no other clue to this fence's identity? Did no one else see him? There must be a description."

"There may be—but for that you will have to ask Willy or one of the others who were there in the house in Carradale. All I know is the kind of car he was driving and his license number."

Esther slowly raised her eyes to his, great dark eyes with depths a man could drown in. Soulful Mediterranean eyes very much like Jasmin's Egyptian ones—though perhaps it would not be wise to tell her that. These eyes searched his carefully, then a slim hand reached out and took a glass and poured a small measure of Old Mortality. Esther downed it briskly and sighed.

"You are a man of many surprises, Tony. Why did you not mention this earlier?"

"Because I forgot, honestly. It has been busy, you know. I heard someone call out about the car and I scratched the information on one of the hundred dollar bills so I wouldn't forget. Here." He groped the wallet from his pocket—then paled. "I cashed the bill with the details on it!"

Tony scrabbled through the bills quickly, turning them about and holding them up to the light, then sighed deeply. "No I didn't, sorry for the scare. I tucked it into the middle of the stack to be safe. Here it is. GRN, that must mean green. Then CAPRI and the number 8463Y. Do you have that?"

"I do. If you will excuse me for a moment I will have Isaj get on the phone with this. We have certain contacts in the police department who will put this in as a routine request for information."

She was back in a moment with a most thoughtful look on her face. "We have just had a report from our stakeout at the colonel's house. A very dirty VW bus is parked there now and five Cubans have entered the house. Do you know anything about this?"

"I certainly do. That's the thing we went to Scotland in. It must be Jorge and the others returning with their tails between their legs because the Scotch grabbed the colonel. They don't know what to do without him."

"Is Jorge the one from the airplane?"

"Right, the second in command of the Cuban skyjackers."

"Is there a chance he might know who the fence might be?"

"Every chance in the world."

"And what he does not know that Jasmin person might. Or someone else in the house. I think the time has come to interview the people there. Would you like to come with us while we talk to them? I must warn you it is completely illegal and might be dangerous."

"Let's go." He laughed hollowly. "Unless we find out who has the money I'll be a wanted criminal on the run for the rest of my life. What's one more charge?"

"That's the spirit. You would make a good international agent if you only put your mind to it."

Bolstered by this dubious compliment, Tony sipped a little more Old Mortality while the wheels of organization began rolling for the raid. A number of scruffy lodgers appeared who, up close, were not that scruffy at all. Jinon and Isaj organized things quickly. Within twenty minutes all was ready and the raiders departed while Esther and Tony hailed a cab and followed at a more leisurely pace.

"Give them a few minutes start," Esther said. "We can arrive after the fireworks are over. We don't want you getting hurt."

Tony waggled his eyebrows rapidly and shook his thumb at the driver, whose large, red cockney ear was just beyond the open partition. A typical London cabbie, thick of neck, strong of jaw, solid as Gibraltar, English to the core.

"Shalom," Esther said.

"Shalom, Estherla," the cabbie answered. "How's your poppa these days?"

"Happy on the kibbutz. He's raising oranges, very proud of them."

"Oranges, yes. Mishugganah Arabs, no. He can keep it. Say hello when you see him."

Whatever the carload of Israeli agents had done had been done swiftly. The cab drove through the darkened streets and stopped before a familiar house, behind an even more familiar VW bus, hijacker transport deluxe. As Tony and Esther walked up the steps the front door opened and Jinon, or perhaps Isaj, waved them in.

"A piece of cake," he announced. "Most of them were asleep when we broke in. We have them in a sort of conference room on the first floor."

The only evidence of forced entry was a splintered gouge next to the lock on the front door and a Marmion bed & breakfast lodger lolling on a settee in the hall with a Bren gun in his lap; he waved to them happily as they climbed the stairs.

"It looks more like the Pentagon war room," Tony said when they entered the board room where the newly captured prisoners were being held. A large and gleaming table, surrounded by chairs, stretched the length of the chamber. Curtained windows covered one long wall, while the facing wall was filled by an immense map of the world. As in the aggrandizing maps and postcards sold to tourists in the great state of Texas, here Cuba had been expanded to match her size in the hearts of her expatriate sons. It loomed, large and green, off the shores of a pallid United States, next to a shriveled Central America, a great and prosperous island about two thirds the size of Africa. From it green streamers—even red tape was not allowed in this bastion of anti-communism—led to all the major capitals of the world. In case this inflation of a simple Caribbean island to world status might be misunderstood, the wall at the far end of the room contained one mighty black-draped, gold-framed portrait of a scowling individual in the uniform of commander of the galaxy armies, or some equivalent rank, who bore a resemblance to the gone but not forgotten Fulgencio Batista. Farther down the wall, to the left of course, was a much smaller portrait, hanging crookedly, of Fidel Castro. It had been used as a target and was pincushioned full of darts, contained a number of bullet holes and was impaled by a steel-tipped hunting arrow.

Relaxed Israelis were standing in the corners of the room, and seated in the chairs around the conference table were six unshaven, red-eyed scowling men and a single equally scowling woman. Jorge looked up and bared his teeth when Tony came in, and then spoke out clearly:

"*¡No te arrugues cuero viejo que te quiero para tambor!*"

"Shut up," Tony suggested. "There are women present and they do not wish to hear that kind of language. Hello, Jasmin."

"*Svinja, cochon, merde . . .*"

"On second thought, maybe they do. When you are through with the language lesson, Jasmin, I want you to tell me what you are doing here with these skyjackers of your plane."

"I tell you nozzing."

"Oh, you can talk a bit of English," Esther said, smiling sweetly. "That's nice."

Both women looked each other up and down swiftly, efficiently, radiating suspicion, examination, hatred, disgust, loathing, all with the use of eyebrows and nostrils and without the use of words. Esther added a lifted shoulder of contempt and the turned back of rejection. Jasmin bit her lips in silence. Tony shook his head ruefully at her.

"You know, at one time I really felt sorry for you. Knocked about by that horrid skyjacker. It was very realistic, I have to admit that. But he knocked you down so you could stay on the plane because you were part of the plot all along. What was your job—getting the weapons aboard in Karachi?"

She turned her face away from him and did not answer. Jorge spoke in her stead, a crisp low-voiced rattle of *barrio* insults that had the other Cubans smirking covertly and craftily, all smarmily describing Tony's female relatives and going back a number of generations.

Fatigue, excitement, strange hours and even stranger drinks had, without his knowledge, tightened Tony to the snapping point. He rarely lost his temper, it was not something he enjoyed, but when he did a hundred generations of pure-blood Apaches raised their heads and war-whooped. In a bound he was across the room and had seized Jorge and hurled him from his chair to the floor, standing over him with fists clenched. Jorge gaped. The anger dimmed and Tony wondered just what to do with the prostrate skyjacker when memory supplied the answer. Hadn't Jorge been happy to hold him when the colonel had pressed the gun to his skull and threatened to pull the trigger? He had, playing right shoulder as Tony remembered.

"You two, pick him up," Tony ordered, waving two of the Israelis forward. He was not aware of their hesitation or Esther's quick nod in their direction. They hauled Jorge to his feet. "A pistol," Tony shouted, his hand out, still glaring at the frightened man. Frightened? Good, keep it going. Esther slapped a pistol into his palm and he pushed the muzzle against Jorge's head.

"Now, you know how this goes. You are going to answer my question. You two—hold him but move aside, don't stand behind him, that's fine. I want to know the name of the fence that the colonel was going to take the skyjacked bills to. I want his name and where I can find him—"

"I don't know!"

"That doesn't matter to me. If you don't know, then you are a dead man. If you do know, you will speak before I say three or I pull the trigger and that is your end. Think of the name, ready. One, two . . ."

"Uncle Tom!" Shouted hoarsely.

"What? You make jokes on your deathbed?"

"No, I swear, on my honor, the name, a store, a pawnshop, not far, Woolwich. I'll give you the address, on Plumstead Common. You can find it."

Tony slowly lowered the gun and turned away, drained. Esther took the gun from him and spoke quietly. "The safety catch was on all the time. Would you have pulled the trigger?"

He shrugged and went and pulled one of the darts from Castro's portrait. "I don't think so. And if I had I would probably have missed. I'm a lousy shot." He hurled the dart at Batista and impaled his left earlobe. "Even with darts. I was aiming at his heart."

"You are a wonderful brave man and there are plenty of killers in the world so you should be happy not to be one. It is more important to be brave, and you will have to be braver still."

"What do you mean?" With a sinking feeling.

"I thought it was obvious. Someone must approach this Uncle Tom with the American bank notes and pretend to be a Cuban trying to sell them, able to speak Spanish and all that. Who but you could do that?"

TWELVE

Esther had all of the arguments ready, Tony had nothing but stammered defenses. The world of the underworld, sinister fences with furtive gunmen, waited close-by. It was a closed book to him and, as far as he was concerned, it would remain forever that way. But opposed to his natural reflexes were all of Esther's sound conclusions. She counted them off on her fingers as she led him from the room and up the stairs again, right up to the top of the house. The only lead they had was Uncle Tom. It was doubtful if information could be forced out of Uncle Tom, so if anything were to be learned it would have to be learned by trickery. Tony would present himself as a Cuban bearing sky-jacked money. Esther and her competent companions would be waiting nearby, ready to intercede in case of difficulties. And, after all, he was the one who was in trouble, wanted by the police, anxious to clear his good name. They would give him all the help they could, but he was the only one who could approach the fence in the needed guise.

"But what do we do with the skyjackers?" he asked, quickly throwing up one more defensive barricade. "The second we leave here Jorge gets in touch with Uncle Tom and I end up in the Thames wearing a concrete overcoat."

"That is no problem." She opened the door at the end of the long hall and showed him in. The light switch was on the wall outside. "Isaj found this. Charming don't you think?"

Here was the colonel's workshop, or hobby room, where he relaxed after a hard day's skyjacking. The door was thick metal, padded on the inside, as were the walls. There were no windows; air came in from heavy metal ducts in the ceiling. There were manacles hanging from all the walls and in the far corner stood a homely umbrella stand filled with whips of various sizes and strengths. Esther looked around disapprovingly.

"Old habits die hard. I suppose no one will tell us if the colonel ever used this charming chamber, but he certainly had it ready for use when the time came. A very not-nice man and we must see to it that he is put away somewhere out of harm's way. Meanwhile we can put all the others in here and they will be secure. You can be sure there is no way out when the door is locked. But we'll check in any case. Once you are through with your conversation with Uncle Tom we can send someone back here to open the door. They are rather awful people, aren't they?"

For some reason the room decided Tony. It reminded him of the colonel and of the tobacconist in Glasgow and stiffened his backbone considerably. "Right. Let's do it before my spirit wilts."

"You are a wonderful man, Tony Hawkin," Esther said, sincere emotion in her voice. She put her slim arms over his shoulders and planted a warm and lingering kiss on his surprised lips. "It is just too bad you aren't Jewish," she whispered into his ear and gave it a gentle bite.

"I'm a comrade in arms," he said, enthusiastically returning the kiss. "I'm the only American Indian FBI man who ever worked for the Israeli underground in Mexico."

"Hush." She put a finger to his lips. "That information is still classified and even I don't know about it."

"You two through yet?" Isaj (or was it Jinon?) asked from the doorway, gun cradled in arms, one world-weary eyebrow raised. "The natives are getting restless downstairs."

"Get them up here and lock them in. We are going to have a look at Uncle Tom."

With many dark glances and muttered complaints, the skyjackers were locked into the colonel's game room. Jasmin protested at being imprisoned with all these men and Esther gave her a knowing look that spoke louder than words. The door was indeed soundproof and capable of being heavily bolted so, with their flank held strongly, the Jewish-Apache raiding party restored weapons to suitcases and shopping bags and left even more quietly than they had entered.

"We'll take the VW too," Jinon (Isaj?) said, holding up the keys. "I liberated them from your friend Jorge."

"But it's a rental car," Tony, for some indecipherable reason, protested.

"Then they'll just have to pay for the extra mileage," Esther told him, with woman's unarguable logic, and they climbed in.

From Tony's point of view the ride was over far too hurriedly. The rush-hour traffic had already swept by so they were able to cross the Thames on a spired bridge with great ease. After that the road led east, with Esther pointing out all the sights, until they slowed to a halt beside a large green area set about with trees, surrounded tightly by buildings. "Plumstead Common," Esther announced. "The shop is on the other side."

"What is that?" Tony asked, pointing at the yellow glow of windows, the colorful blazon of arms above.

"A pub, as you very well know."

"I do know. I intend to take you there for a drink while your forces get into position, then you will lead me to the door and slip away. Is it a deal?"

"You are very brave. It is a deal."

The door moved easily under Tony's hand to reveal a humming, low-ceilinged chamber filled with strong tobacco smoke, which instantly set him to coughing, and crowded with men almost shoulder to shoulder. There were a few women at tiny tables on the periphery, most of them past their prime, all industriously talking, but it was the men who dominated the establishment. They seemed uniformly dressed in tan raincoats that were stained in similar patterns, and wore caps pulled low over their eyes or, pushed back as the case may be. Leading Esther by the hand, Tony pushed through the pack and managed to make the haven of the bar, where he clutched to the rounded wooden edge while he fought hard to catch the eye of one of the laboring bartenders. Both were well-muscled and white-shirted, pumping hard on the beer handles and sending forth a steady stream of large full glasses. One of them finally noticed Tony's frantic waving, perhaps his beer-pump arm was tired, though that did not seem possible, and he came over with a wet rag, which he used to spread the pools of beer into a sort of counter-top-wide lake.

"Wargh?" he said, or something like that, which Tony took to mean that he was ready to be commanded; the heady sound of many men's voices made conversation difficult.

"We'd like to order some drinks. What do you want, Esther?"

"Ginenit," she said loudly and the bartender nodded.

"Whisky. A large whisky. I mean two large whiskies in one glass."

"Dutch courage?" Esther shouted conversationally. He showed her his teeth in a spastic grin. "No, just the desire to have a big drink because it has been a long time since I had one and it will probably be an even longer time until the next."

"I am sorry, I really did intend it as a joke. Perhaps my sense of humor has gone off after that horrible house."

"Mine too. I shouldn't have snapped. For a secret agent you are very easy to love."

"What? I didn't hear you, the noise."

"I said shalom. Isn't that what you say? I never found out what it meant."

"It means peace. As in peace pipe."

"I'll drink to that."

They did and the drinks were gone all too quickly, then they were outside in the cool air, cooled even more by an insinuating drizzle that was blowing over the distant chimneys and sweeping across the grass toward them. On the next street corner was a glass-fronted establishment with indecipherable objects concealed behind the nightblind and dusty windows.

"That's the place," Esther said. "Doesn't look open." Tony answered, cooled by the rain and depressed by the onslaughts of fatigue. "Of course it's closed, but he obviously lives over the shop. Hammer on the door until he answers. I'm sure he does most of his clandestine business after dark." She slipped away. Tony took a deep breath and strode forward, went to the dark entrance and tapped lightly. The door opened instantly and someone hissed at him until he went in. A shaded light was turned on.

"You're not Stanley. Who're you?"

"Can we be overheard?" Tony whispered, Cuban accent thick, looking around suspiciously. They were in a darkened showroom filled with the castoff and unredeemed debris of countless households. Andirons and bent pokers clanged at his feet, an upholstered couch bled its stuffing over garish reproductions of bad paintings set in chipped frames. A set of battered golf clubs, half of them undoubtedly missing, lay on top of an unstrung piano next to a brace of warped guitars. More and more dismal objects vanished into the gloom above and on all sides, mercifully concealed by the darkness. Whatever business was done here was certainly not done with these rejected castoffs. The proprietor had the same castoff look as his goods, a gray and wrinkled man of indifferent age, his skin hanging loosely on his slight frame as though it were someone else's, taken in pawn like the rest of his goods. His trousers were shapeless, his vest hung limply over a badly wrinkled shirt, his steel-rimmed glasses rode low on his pointed nose; he looked so disheveled and miserable that he must be very rich.

"Look, who are you? Speak up or nip out."

"I am looking for Uncle Tom."

"Well you've found him. Business hours nine to five, later by appointment, now 'op it."

"But I am here by appointment about *dinero,* something green and crackling, on the orders of a certain colonel who shall remain nameless unless you wish the name."

Uncle Tom seemed slightly taken aback by the news. He was silent, still, only his eyes flicking up and down Tony's form, a single index finger moving as well, scratching at his side, perhaps unseating some unwanted form of life. Before he could reach any decision there was a faint tapping at the door.

"In that corner, keep your gob shut." Uncle Tom hurried to the entrance while Tony settled uncomfortably onto a horsehair chair, the seat of which contained a broken spring that probed sharply upward with hopes of making an intramuscular injection. The door opened and closed quickly and a small man appeared under the shaded light with a dark bundle. Uncle Tom peered at it suspiciously and they conversed demotically in voices rich with glottal stops and unusual diphthongs.

"You 'ave it?"

"Arr. First class, five quid at least."

"Plated, dented, I'll give you three."

"Bloody hell, I'll bung 'em in river first. Four."

"Three pound fifty, out of the goodness of me heart."

"My arse, you got no 'art, Uncle. It's a deal."

The package was passed over and bank notes rustled. Uncle Tom put the package in a dark corner, no shortage of them, and hissed Tony out of his. Before he could speak a phone began ringing in the distance. Muttering to himself, the master of the establishment found his way unerringly through the looming piles and answered it. The conversation, mostly monosyllabic mutters and grunts from his end, was blissfully short, Tony was getting edgy with the waiting and interruptions, and they picked up where they had left off.

"All right, what's his name?" Uncle Tom asked.

"Who?"

"Who? The bleeding colonel, that's who."

"Colonel Juarez-Sedoño."

"Arumm. But he said the whole thing was off for a bit, had to wait."

"The waiting is over."

"Got the lolly, hey? Why didn't he say so?"

"I am saying so for him since he is away on a business trip to Scotland. Do you want to see it or not?"

"I don't know, a pretty big deal, I was never happy." His eyes blinked rapidly and his ears twitched as Tony took out the bundle of hundred dollar bills and rustled them through his fingers. "Over under the light."

Tony flipped the bundle again, then pulled out one of the bills and passed it over. Uncle Tom produced from his vest a jeweler's loupe, which he screwed into his eye, through which he examined the bill closely on both sides, up and down and back and forth. Then he crinkled it, smelled it, tasted it with the tip of his tongue and handed it back.

"Real all right, but marked eight different ways." So much for scientific undetectability. "Not easy to get rid of anything like this." The phone rang again and he shuffled off. Tony put the money away and made an invisible cat's cradle with his fingers through another ahrring and humming phone call until the fence returned.

"I don't like it," Uncle Tom said, blinking a suspicious and fishy eye at Tony. "It's too big a job for me to lay off alone. It has to be got out of the country and there is only one lad for that job. You see him and see what he says and if he says that what he says goes then I says it might be possible." Tony labored through the syntax and extracted the nugget of information at its core.

"Who is this I have to see?"

"Man named Massoud. He runs a restaurant on the Portobello Road, name of The Taj Mahal. Next to the Mucky Duck, you can't miss it. See him and see what he says."

There was no more information forthcoming because, as he spoke, Uncle Tom had a hand in the small of Tony's back and was hustling him to the door and out. Tony protested but could think of nothing more to say, so he permitted himself to be pushed through and heard the lock being turned behind him. Esther was waiting around the corner and nodded at his information.

"I think I know the place. The Mucky Duck is a common aphorism for any public house named the Black Swan. We must go, but we must have a plan. This address is on the other side of London and it will take at least a half an hour to get there.

I'll go in the first car, the fast one, and you follow in that rented thing. I will be there having dinner with Isaj and we will not recognize each other. If there is trouble we will be ready. The others can go back to the Marmion."

"But it's after ten at night, the restaurant won't be open." Hopefully spoken, instantly dashed.

"This is a fine hour for an Indian restaurant. We will be waiting when you arrive."

There was no escaping the workings of fate. He sat next to Jinon, it had to be him since Isaj was with Esther, who drove on the way back, and was regaled with fascinating stories of midnight raids on infiltrators' positions, hearty climbs up the heights of Masada in hundred-degree heat, friendly nights around the bonfire at the kibbutz, horseback riding at dawn in the barren hills as well as other healthy and exhausting Israeli pursuits. It was so enthusiastic that, had he been Jewish, Tony would have emigrated instantly; only his Apache blood saved him from a happy life as a kibbutznik. London streamed past and, all too soon, he had to once more become the double—or was it triple?—agent.

"Good luck," Jinon called after him as he started down the road toward the beckoning restaurant sign. "And shalom."

Shalom indeed, Tony muttered to himself; if there were more shalom in the world he would not be in the position he was in now. He passed the alcoholic temptations of the Black Swan and stopped to examine the menu posted in the window of the Taj Mahal. An endless variety of strange dishes was listed with prices for each, ending in a brief addition of steak, chicken and eggs served with chips, sop to the unexperimental British eater. A round exhaust fan was mounted above the entrance door, where it hurled rich waves of spiced Eastern cookery into the gasoline-fumed night air. It was all totally unfamiliar, but strangely attractive despite that, so that Tony's salivary glands, ever alert for opportunity, pumped a quick spurt into his mouth to show their interest. He took a deep breath and entered.

Beyond the door was a single large room with numerous small, white-tableclothed tables. The walls, and the ceiling, were imaginatively covered with red plush-flocked wallpaper, the plush worn thin over the tables where industriously working elbows of diners had scrubbed it away. Yellow bulbs glowed dimly on the half-dozen customers who were attacking steaming dishes and glowing mounds of rice. The two Israelis were among them and he let his eyes slide over them as easily as the other customers. A dark-skinned waiter appeared and waved him toward a table.

"Would you like to dine, sah?"

Well why not? It had been twenty-four hours since he had had a real meal and if the food here tasted anything like it smelled he was going to enjoy it. Certainly the Israelis were. Then stern duty laid a heavy hand on his shoulder and he sighed inwardly at an opportunity missed.

"No, I'm here to see someone by the name of Massoud."

"I'm sorry but he is busily occupied at moment, however I will tell him you are here. If you will wait here it will be some minutes. Perhaps some tea or something to drink while you wait?"

Reprieve! "Drink, yes, but I want something to eat as well." He sat at the nearest table and rested his elbows on the yellow stains of the tablecloth and seized the menu. It was indecipherable. "What do you recommend tonight?" The standard gambit of the unknowing.

"Madras beef is very good, but very hot, so you must like hot food."

"I like hot food that is *caliente* hot and *picante* hot both. Do you mean spicy hot, not stove hot?"

"Quite right, from the red chilies."

"I'll have it."

"Madras beef dinner with brinjal pickle paratha onion baji tarka dahl rice pilaf bombay duck to start."

"I don't like duck. Do you have beer?"

"Bombay duck is fish. And one lager."

This was more like it. The lager proved to be a glass of warm beer, which he sipped with the food that instantly began to appear, course after course. It was all good, and he washed it down with more lager, his mission completely forgotten in this furious stoking of his appetite. He was sweating heavily and mopping up a last bit of sauce with a shred of paratha when a tall man appeared at his elbow.

"I am Massoud. You wish to see me?" Gold teeth flashed warmly against the mocha of his skin; his eyes were as cold and unrevealing as a snake's. Tony hurriedly washed down the last mouthful of food with the remains of his beer.

"Yes, if I could."

"There is privacy in the upstairs dining room, this way if you please."

A dark staircase lay beyond the dumbwaiter, from which waiters were still extracting food from the kitchen in the cellar below, shouting incomprehensible commands down the shaft. On the floor above they passed doors labeled LADIES and GEN-TLEMENS, linguistic traps lurk everywhere in English, and on to the door at the far end.

"Here, please, I will turn on the light."

The light came on, Massoud stood in the doorway behind him, and Tony faced into the small room already well filled with people, all familiar, the two most familiar of all sitting at the table and facing him. Smiling?

Willy MacGregor and Colonel Juarez-Sedoño.

THIRTEEN

It was one of those nightmare situations, the sort of thing one dreams about and then happily awakes to reality. Except that Tony was awake and this was no dream. He recoiled automatically from that loathsome twosome and fell back against Massoud's arm. *Out* his reflexes screamed at him, and out seemed a very good idea to his conscious mind as well. Massoud clutched at him but he evaded the grasping fingers by ducking under them, rushing back down the hall, diving at the staircase, leaping down three, four, five steps at a time, risking everything in the need for flight. His stomach, stuffed with curry and rice, felt heavy as a bowling ball behind his belt, slowing him, but not that much. Out was very much the order and he was getting out.

He stumbled at the foot of the stairs, almost fell, had a quick glimpse of wide-eyed waiters and interested customers, Esther looking at him with startled eyes.

"Get out!" he shouted. "The colonel's upstairs."

Setting a good example, he pounded toward the front door but two customers sitting next to it were there first. Big men in rough tweeds who stood before the exit and turned to face him. Were those bicycle chains swinging from their lumpy fists? Tony slowed to a trot, to a halt, then collapsed into a chair. There was a pitcher of water on the table before him so he filled a glass and drained it. Things were not turning out just as expected. Willy came down the stairs and crooked a finger in his direction.

"Now if you are through with that sort of thing you can come back upstairs. You two as well." He stabbed a blunt finger at Esther and Isaj, who rose slowly. Isaj dropped his hand casually into his coat pocket and Willy called out sharply, "None of that. The last real customer left here ten minutes ago."

It was true. The waiters arose from the kitchen with carving knives, the cook emerged behind them with a cleaver, while the remaining pseudo-clients turned cold northern eyes toward the Israelis, bicycle chains gliding from their pockets.

"They're pretty fast with those things," Tony called out. "I think you better listen to him, Isaj."

For a long instant the Israeli agent glared around at the advancing men, as though counting heads and counting bullets and doing a sum. The answer was not too good. In the end he shrugged and smiled, then tossed a small automatic onto the table. The nearest chain wielder scooped it up. Willy nodded.

"Much better. Now—everyone upstairs."

It was crowded in the private dining room above, but no one noticed. Willy and the colonel were seated behind the table once again, with Tony and the two Israeli agents facing them, as though prisoners before the bar. Indians and Scots were around the walls, with one uncomfortable-looking Cuban, Jorge, in their midst. It was a grim gathering indeed.

"Well now," Willy said, steepling his fingers before him on the table in schoolmaster fashion, metal-rimmed glasses glinting. "I have a few questions for you, Mr. Hawkin. The colonel here swears on his honor that you know where the money is."

"He's a liar."

"Really? You told me that once before—but you also had some of the skyjacked notes with you at the time. Yes, still there? Uncle Tom reported their existence. That's better, just reach into your pocket slowly and hand them over. A good beginning —now where are the rest?"

"I have no idea. That's all I have and I took them from the colonel."

"I find that hard to believe. If you are so innocent, why did you visit Uncle Tom tonight and offer to sell him the rest of the money? It is only by chance that we interceded in time. The colonel and I have reached an impasse and a sort of agreement. Therefore we returned to London earlier this evening and were unpleasantly shocked to find all of the colonel's men imprisoned in his own house. Jorge revealed your interest in Uncle Tom and we took it from there . . ."

"The second phone call."

"Correct. Since Massoud here was to be involved in the transport of the money, and also feels hurt at being cheated, we arranged for everyone to meet here. Now, all the parties involved in this matter are gathered together and anxious to resolve it. I ask you again—and for the last time—where is the money?"

There was taut silence then, broken only by the squeak of an unoiled bicycle chain, and Tony looked around the room. Where *was* the money? All of the interested parties seemed to be in this room. The Al Fatah agent who had arranged for the weapons, the Scots and Cubans who had skyjacked the plane, the fence who was to take care of the money, the FBI agent who had delivered the money, the Israeli agents who had helped the FBI man who had delivered the money to the . . .

He stopped and shook his head. It was all here—or was it? One piece was still missing, one element. What?

Then, in a single clang of insight, the rolling steel ball of memory dropped through the hole in the pinball machine of logic and all of the lights lit up. Of course!

Tony looked about the room again and smiled sweetly at the glowering assemblage. He held his hand before him and examined his nails, then buffed them on his arm. "I think I can answer that question," he said. "But I would like a few promises first."

"I promise to cut your swinish throat from ear to ear," the colonel hinted.

"Tell him to shut up or I won't go on," Tony said to Willy. "He's a liar and I can prove it. That bundle of money I took from him was brought to him from the plane by Jorge there, taken out of the suitcase before Angus spirited it away. I heard Ramon tell him it was for the fence. Go ahead—ask Jorge if that isn't true."

"He doesn't speak English."

"Then have the colonel ask him. I'll sort of listen to the colonel to make sure he asks the right question. Go on colonel."

Juarez-Sedoño hurled a poison-dripping glare at Tony but had no choice once the bicycle chains began to whistle ominously. Jorge had heard his name mentioned and was pallid with fear, only too willing to nod in agreement when the question was put to him. Tony nodded as well.

"Good. Now we know that the colonel was lying and I don't have the money. Am I permitted to ask what agreement you came to with him?"

"A simple one," Willy said. "We both agreed that Angus was a little greedy in trying to take all the money for the Scots' cause, noble as that cause be. It was decided that we work together to recover the money, then take the fifty-fifty split originally agreed upon. Though I don't know now, the colonel is such a crafty one."

"It was agreed, we shook hands," the colonel said.

"We did and I'll abide by it because I'm a man of honor even when dealing with a snake. Continue, Hawkin."

"Right. The only lead any of us had to the identity of the thief and killer was the fact it was a fence. I heard you say that, Willy. That's why I went to see Uncle Tom. It was a dead end—in more ways than one. The only other clue we have is the license number of the car the killer escaped in."

"Aye, we're still working on that. It's not easy."

"It's easy enough for us," Esther said, her clear voice cutting through the thick air and causing all the heads to swivel in her direction. "We have better contacts than you have. The police. We have friends. We didn't say why but we had them search the records. The answer came in a little while ago—after we parted, Tony," she said in his direction, smiling. "It's simple. There is no such number registered in the British Isles."

A miasma of gloom settled on the crowded room; the trail was growing murkier all the time. "We have another clue," Tony said. "Didn't anyone see the murderer when he arrived?"

"We all did," Willy muttered. "It was a man, I guess, for all we could tell. Dark trousers, dark boots, a Ganex mac, dark hat, scarf around his face, dark glasses, average height, average build, plenty of clothes on, couldn't tell a thing. Could have been the Queen herself for all we knew."

"Let's eliminate suspects then." Tony ticked them off on his fingers. "It wasn't Willy because I was in the room next door with him. The colonel had fainted by the dock and the rest of the Cubans were hightailing it out of town. The Israelis didn't know about Scotland yet."

"What about *her?*" the colonel shouted, stabbing a finger in Jasmin's direction. "She could have done it."

Jasmin quailed. "Nevair! I was in beauty parlor all that afternoon."

"A weak alibi." The colonel flared his nostrils and glared monoptically.

"But a true one," Esther said sweetly. "We were trailing this Egyptian cow and, for all the good it did, that's where she was all right."

Tony waited until the screamed insults subsided before he continued. "That takes care of everyone in this room other than Massoud."

"I was cooking banquet! Ask the happy customers I served. It is not my way, I do not do this sort of thing, I receive, pay cash, sell, a businessman simply."

"It could have been another fence," Willy said.

"Never! We do not do that, and no one knew but Uncle Tom and I. No one else in this country would touch a thing like this, no one knew . . ."

"I tend to agree with Massoud," Tony said. "He wasn't the one who did it. It was someone else. And I think I know who." He had their attention now, oh yes he did. Then why was he sweating? He knew perfectly well why he was sweating. If this didn't work there would be the swish of bicycle chains, the bark of guns. Don't think about that! "I said I *think* I know who, but before I tell you I want a deal . . ."

"No deals," Colonel Juarez-Sedoño shouted. "If he knows I can get it out of him. Someone hand me a gun, even a whip."

Willy made a gesture with his hand and one of the Scots

pushed the colonel back into his chair, where he frothed noisily. "What kind of a deal are you thinking of?"

"A cut, a small cut, that's all. That money was put up by the United States Government on the promise of a number of Arab governments to pay them back. They have paid, all except one holdout, so the U.S. is two hundred thousand dollars short. That's all I want out of the two million—you can split the rest. I'll return that to the States so our records will be clear and the rest of the money will be someone else's problem. I'm not sure that my superiors will approve of this arrangement so I don't plan to tell them. I don't think you will either. This is between us, you and I, Willy. You have my word that I'll tell you everything I know and will lead you to the money—if you promise me my share."

Willy thought for a moment, then nodded his head. "That seems reasonable enough—if you do have the information. You have my word on it."

"That's good enough by me. Now I ask the important question. Who haven't we considered? The missing person?" He looked around at their blank stares and raised a tutorial finger. "We have been too busy thinking about a fence being the culprit because we were deliberately *led* to think that. What made you think a fence was there that afternoon, Willy?"

"Why—Angus himself told me."

"And Angus got you into this plot in the first place. He also involved the colonel and I'll bet he was the one who contacted Jasmin. Now, knowing Angus as well as you do, do you think he was the sort of man who could come up with a complex international scheme like this, then pull it off?"

"Well, he was a good Scots patriot."

"I'm sure of it. But the police think of him as a small-time thug as well. Isn't it just possible that he was acting as the front man for *someone else*? The secret master behind this entire scheme. Garcia may have known who this was as well, which is why Angus killed him. Then Angus was killed in return to keep the secret a secret forever. Who is that person? It becomes sort of obvious when we remember that there was someone else in Scotland the day of the murder. Someone very closely involved with the entire skyjacking . . ."

"*Me lleva a la tisnada!*" The colonel was beating his clenched fists on the table; Tony smiled upon him beneficently.

"See, the colonel remembers and he is excoriating himself for not having thought of it sooner . . ."

"The pilot of the aircraft!" the colonel moaned.

Tony looked around with appreciation at the open mouths of incomprehension that gaped about the room. "Let me explain. Early in the morning of the killing the colonel and I had breakfast with Captain Haycroft at the train station in Glasgow. He seemed put out to see me there and did not want to talk to the colonel. He ate quickly and hurried away. In plenty of time to obtain a car and some kind of false license plates, undoubtedly already arranged, to get to Carradale ahead of us. And do you know what he said he was doing in Scotland? Looking through the mug books to see if he could identify any of the skyjackers. He said the police had sent him there. But I had seen many more of the men who got the money from the car and Scotland Yard only asked *me* to look at the books they had in London. Which means Haycroft was lying."

"It is possible, very possible," Willy agreed. "The captain knew the route of the ship and could make all necessary arrangements. He might have checked the airfield to see if he could land his aircraft. Then he did find it and land it safely. He was in the position to arrange and supervise the whole thing from under cover, even have his own hostess employed where he could watch her."

"He did it!" Jasmin shouted, jumping to her feet. "All the time so noble, the *cochon*. I was told to get the arms into the locked rest room, that was all, and I did so. Yet the captain was the one who found it inoperable and he locked it himself. We must take him, make him reveal the money, Al Fatah will have its share—we did our part, we were promised."

"We will divide the money once we have it in our hands," Willy judged, Solomon-like. "Where is the captain now?"

Jasmin pointed to the shrouded window. "There, with the airplane. He stays nearby and supervises the arrangements to remove the ship. I can show you the house—for our share."

"That will be discussed in private, and the same goes for you, Massoud. I imagine you still want to fence the notes?"

"You are mad!" Massoud said, backing away and pushing back invisible money. "I will not touch it! Everyone knows, the FBI, the Israelis, it will be shouted from street corners soon, I am out of business forever and, P.S., a fine curry restaurant is for sale cheap since I return to Calcutta tonight. . . ."

"All right, don't get excited," Willy cozened. "Just keep your mouth shut about this business and we'll all do the same. We're getting out of here now and we're going down to Kent to pay a call on the captain. And I'm warning all of you not to play any of your Arabic-Jewish-Cuban-American tricks. My boys will be watching you closely for the cause of bonny Scotland." Murmured *ochs* and *ayes* and rattled bicycle chains echoed his words. "Right then, all understood. We'll move out now, a few at a time, a couple of the lads will be close to each of you."

Three by three they went slowly from the Taj Mahal, each shrinking foreigner shepherded by two steely-eyed and iron-thewed sons of Caledonia. The presence in central London of all these magnificently muscled Scots was explained when they emerged and found a great long bus at the curb outside, single-decked and sleek, high-wheeled and shining. Painted down the side in bold letters was the legend LOCH LOMOND TOURS (SCOTLAND) LTD. The driver gave Willy a toothless grin and a thumbs-up salute as they boarded. Willy looked grim nevertheless.

"It's the money," he confided in Tony. "Yon Sandy got us the commercial discount on the coach, but it's still bloody expensive hiring it for the trip. But I needed all the laddies here to stand behind me, me being a man of intellect and not of brawn. You're not lying to me, are you, Hawkin? Or God help me, you'll rue this day."

"Why lie? This looks like the only way out for all of us. Find the boss behind the skyjacking and get the money from him. Is there anything else we can do?"

There appeared to be nothing. Massoud locked the restaurant as they filed out and hurried away, eyes averted, perhaps never to return. Sandy closed the door behind the last of them and pulled out into the lamplit streets of midnight London. Probably by reflex, he flicked a switch and they hummed down the road soothed by the melodious recorded strains of bagpipe music. Tony went to sit by Esther.

"I'm sorry I got you into this," he said.

"Don't be silly, this is my business. And I did promise to keep an eye on you, a job I'm not doing too well at the present time."

"It's not your fault and, you should pardon my asking, what is a pretty girl like you doing in a business like this?"

"Don't ask. It all came about by accident. I grew up in London and New York, my father is a correspondent for a big Tel-Aviv newspaper, so my English is transatlantic and not bad at all."

"It's perfect."

"You're very sweet. Anyway, I was at university here and they needed some help and they asked me—so I helped. No one knows I'm Israeli unless I tell them, so I can get in places, hear things, talk to people. And once it started it sort of kept on. Instead of having me do my national service in the army I stayed on in London and one thing led to another. Now I work for my father's paper and that is that. Now tell me how you got into the FBI. You don't seem like some of the FBI agents we see in the films."

"I don't seem like any of the agents you see in the FBI!"

It was a priceless opportunity to tell someone his troubles and he seized it with both hands. School, the army, more school, the National Gallery, the draft to the FBI, the Mexican assignment, she squeezed his hand at the exciting parts, the FBI again and finally the skyjacking. And while he talked London and the suburbs fell behind them and they rushed down a motorway under a moonlit sky. He had barely finished all the interesting details of the tale when the bus slowed and pulled off the motorway into an internal combustion hell of burning orange lights, rumbling trailer trucks and looming tankers. All of this mechanical action was centered around a windowed building that bore the proud legend FOOD DRINK PETROL, apparently all served from the same font. Willy, suddenly cast in the role of tour guide, stood at the front of the bus with microphone in hand and addressed them through the PA system.

"This is a trucker stop and we're going to stay here for the rest of the night. The field at Tilbury Hill is only about an hour from here and we don't want to go in there with this pantechnicon at this time of night. No one is to leave the coach except my lads. If any of the others have to use the facilities they will be escorted. I suggest we get some sleep—there will be guards so no tricks. And no talking so those that want to sleep can. That is all."

Tony and Esther whispered for a few moments while the coachload of disparate elements settled down, then guttural shhhhs sent them into silence. Tony looked out of the window for a bit, wondering what the morning would bring, resisted the temptation to chew his fingernails until, finally, he fell asleep as well.

FOURTEEN

Gray dawn sent fingers of fog licking into the bus when the door was opened, promoting a chorus of coughs that sounded like the chain smokers' corner of hell. Tony, who had finally fallen into an imitation of restful sleep, was dragged awake by this hacking accompanied by Willy's electronically amplified voice. It was all too much like the army; there should be a reveille formation next. There wasn't, but there was a military organization. Prisoners and guards paraded back and forth, to and from the rest rooms, performing their morning ablutions, hacking heavily as they inhaled the rich mixture of fog and diesel fumes. Soon tea, coffee and sweet cakes that made the teeth glow appeared and were consumed. Despite Willy's nagging insistence to hurry, this took the good part of an hour and the orange globe of the sun was above the hills and burning away the fog before the bus rumbled to life and swung back onto the motorway.

Green England whirred by, then moved by a good deal closer and much slower when they turned off onto the local roads. At each turning the road became narrower until the bus filled it from side to side, brushing leaves from the trees above. There were cows in the fields, orchards in bloom, acres of glistening hop vines twining up their poles. With infinite care the long coach inched over a narrow and ancient bridge in obedience to the sign that indicated that Tilbury Hill was only a mile farther away. Jasmin stood by the driver, giving directions, excitedly pointing to a totally undistinguished semidetached house done in temperance gray stucco; the sign on the gate read DUN ROAMIN. "That is it, where the Captain Haycroft stays."

The ponderous vehicle lurched down the track and came to a stop around a bend. Willy and two of his heavies got out quickly and strolled back along the road. In a few minutes they came hurrying back, all eyes upon them as they climbed in.

"Gone to the airfield already, the woman said. Some sort of construction work going on. We'll take him there."

Air brakes whooshed and away they went. This part of the road was well marked, though the signs were thirty years old at least . . . memories of flaring exhausts in the night, rumble of engines as the bombers took off to bomb Germany. Fading memories now. Yet there was life in the old field yet. They overtook a concrete truck, its massive, motley striped tube of mix turning slowly as it rumbled majestically along. A gate opened wide to admit it, then closed before the bus.

"No coach tours here," an official voice said. Their way was blocked by the solid blue form of the gatekeeper, undoubtedly the man from Fangs and Truncheons that Captain Haycroft had mentioned. The truncheon wasn't in sight, but the fangs certainly were, for at the end of a short lead held in the guard's right hand was the straining form of a low-slung and sinister police dog. It was fat—or musclebound—its figure very much like that of its master, which filled the amply cut uniform. Willy climbed down, keeping an anxious eye on the dog.

"I have business with Captain Haycroft."

"Sorry, sir, no orders about you." The softness of his words were belied by the ugly animal, which yawned and revealed an incredible number of pointed and yellow teeth. Two of the muscular Scotsmen exited and stood behind Willy.

"I must insist," Willy said, feeling the reassurance of his assistants. "It is imperative that I see the captain at once."

The guard, stern face professionally expressionless, did not speak. But he did let out about three extra feet of leash. The dog, which had been straining constantly against its harness, instantly surged forward, with its lips drawn back to clearly reveal the rows of fangs. Willy recoiled with a whinny of fear, falling against his companions, who almost all went down like a row of tenpins. Before things got any worse Tony left the bus as well, taking his wallet from his hip pocket.

"Good morning, Officer, fine day for outside work. My name is Hawkin of the FBI, here is my identification. You may recall from the news reports that I arrived on this plane and am still involved in this case. I must see the captain."

"Yes, sir, go right through." The canine monster was withdrawn and the gate opened wide enough to admit him; Tony felt the informatory jab of Willy's finger in his back.

"These three gentlemen are private investigators from Scotland. They have information for the captain."

Truncheons looked at them coldly and fangs growled deep in his throat. "They can go if you vouch for them, sir, but no more. I would appreciate it if that coach pulled onto the verge, more lorries coming."

"Very good, Officer," Tony said and turned to wave the bus back, speaking quietly to Willy. "We'll talk to Haycroft, then the others can come in."

"Aye."

The gate clanged shut behind them and the mixed foursome strolled onto the airfield. It was far busier now than the day the plane had landed. Trucks lumbered to the far end of the field where men were busily at work on the runway. The DC-10 was still where it had landed but had changed greatly. All of its large hatches were open and a truck, lifted high on jacks, was backed up to it. A construction of large jacks and steel supports held up the wings, and one of the landing gear had been removed. As they passed the spiderweb of supports a man in a coverall looked down on them.

"Hello, Hawkin," he called out. "What are you doing back here at the scene of the crime?" It was Tubby Waterbury, the copilot, with grease on his face and a large flashlight clutched in his hand.

"Still on the case, Tubby. Where's the captain?"

"In the cabin and in a lousy mood. Good luck." He put head and light back into the gaping opening in the wing.

A borrowed landing stairs, labeled TRANS-SAHARA AIRLINES, stood by the plane now and they climbed up it to the open door above. The lofty cabin was shockingly empty with most of the seats gone. Workingmen were carrying the last of them out the door on the far side to the elevated truck body beyond. Captain Haycroft, his back turned, was watching this operation keenly as the men left and the truck sank from sight. He turned when Tony called out to him.

"What brings you here, Hawkin? I thought the police wanted to see you—"

"That's been straightened out," Tony broke in, hurriedly. "Look, Jasmin is here, and some other people, but the guard at the gate won't let them in."

"Quite right, too, the place is crawling with sightseers and gawpers. I'll write a note for the guard."

"Just give permission for the coach to come through," Willy said.

"Just who the hell are you?" Haycroft said, sharply, looking at Willy and his hulking companions. He gave no indication that he had ever seen them before. A very cool one, Tony thought. "That's okay, they're with me," he said aloud. "Could we have the note, please?"

Haycroft glowered a bit longer, then took a pad from his pocket, scrawled on it and tore off the sheet and handed it to Tony. One of the Scotchmen hurried away with it. "What's going on here?" Tony asked, looking around the plane, scratching for a neutral topic until the others arrived. An angry snort from the captain proved he had touched on a theme close to his heart.

"What's going on? Everything, that's what. I've never seen so much confusion in my life. Everyone's been here, insurance people, government, aviation authorities—even a parliamentary investigating committee. It appears that getting this craft out won't be as easy as bringing it in, not that the landing was all that easy. There have been some wild schemes, believe me, but all of them impractical. Even if the plane is taken into a thousand pieces there is no way to get it out by road. There isn't a chopper made that's big enough to lift out the pieces either. So—fly it out. But how? You saw what happened to the runway when we landed. That's when the engineers began with their busy fingers on the slide rules and calculators and came up with this joker of a plan. It's going to take a couple of hundred thousand to do but the insurance company would rather pay that than pay everything and sell the plane for scrap. Take a look out there."

They obediently followed the pointing finger through the open doorway and down the rutted runway to the far end where the machines and men labored.

"First they patch the entire length of the runway. When this is done and the concrete has cured they are going to lay steel matting over it, the kind they used for temporary airfields during the war. This will spread the aircraft's weight around, but not enough. So they are stripping the plane, seats, ovens, lockers, johns, everything not needed. All the fuel, too, except for enough to get us to Heathrow Airport. Then the Air Force is loaning some landing gear from a C-5A with eight wheels each. I won't be able to retract them, but they'll lighten the load per wheel. Theoretically all of this should add up to enough for us to get airborne without going through the runway again or plowing into the cows in that field."

"Will it really work?" Tony asked.

"Your guess is as good as mine. There's enough runway for a takeoff as long as the wheels don't drop through again. They offered me a bonus of twenty grand to fly it out, the same for Tubby, but we're holding out for forty each. What a way to make a living. What the hell is this, the theaters just let out?"

In slow procession the occupants of the coach, now parked on the runway below, were climbing to the plane. Scowling Egyptian, grim Cuban, dour Scot, calm Israeli, one by one they came through the door and spread in a semicircle facing the captain. Tubby popped through the door after them waving his flashlight and calling out cheerily:

"Listen, Haycroft, if you are taking tours through the ship I want a cut of the ticket sales."

"Hawkin! What is the meaning of this damn invasion of my aircraft?"

"You sound so angry, Captain. Do you mean it? I'll bet you know everyone here, though."

"You have exactly sixty seconds to explain just what the devil you are talking about before I boot your rump, and your buddies', right back down the stairs. Jasmin—can you tell me what this is all about?"

"Peeg!" she spat in his direction.

"Hold on, please," Tony asked. "Let's play this cool. Haycroft, we're here about the skyjacked money. I am sure I won't be telling you anything you don't know already, but I want you to know that *we* know everything. You see the entire game is over. It started in Karachi when you locked the rear rest room that *you* said was out of order—"

"Said! The pump was broken and the stuff was right up to there!"

"Please, let me finish. Then Jasmin had the Al Fatah arms loaded aboard and locked in the rest room. The Cubans, and your former friend Angus, were waiting in the transit lounge in the Los Angeles airport. They boarded and skyjacked the plane with the hidden weapons and you flew it here. Then the skyjackers split up in two cars—but the treacherous game wasn't over yet. Angus and his men jumped the Cubans and got all the money away from them, killing Garcia at the same time, undoubtedly because he *knew too much*. We are getting close to the end now because the money was taken from Angus soon after, and he was killed then for the same reason that Garcia was. He knew far too much. He knew the identity of the secret master, the devilish warped mind behind the entire plot, the man who had organized everything and who, in the end, wanted all of the money to himself. Wouldn't you agree that is how it went, Haycroft?"

As Tony had been talking Haycroft had been backing slowly

away, his eyes moving quickly from one to the other of the variegated audience. "Hawkin," he said hoarsely, "I think you are out of your ever-loving mind. Will you kindly just take all your friends and leave?"

"Not good enough, Captain. Because we *know.* We know who the secret master is. You were in Scotland that day, remember? I saw you in the train station with your hokey story about looking at mug photos. Well I know better now, Haycroft. I know that that story was not only a lie but that *you* are the secret master! Where is the money? Hand it over, quickly, because these are desperate men—and women."

Haycroft was at the open door where the truck had been, able to go no farther, his back to the twenty-foot drop. His expression was calm, controlled, his voice steady as only a professional pilot's can be during an emergency. But his forehead was beaded with sweat.

"That's a fine theory, yes, very good. You'll rise to the highest ranks of the FBI with police work like this. It all makes sense, everything—except the fact that I did the job. I did not. I was with the police that entire day, until they took me to the train for the return trip. Call Scotland Yard and they will verify that in two minutes. So it looks like you have the wrong man."

"No!" Tony said. "It *had* to be you."

"Sorry," a new voice said. "But he's not the guilty party. The captain is correct. He was with the police in Glasgow all that day."

As though following a masterful stroke in some invisible tennis game, every head snapped about and looked toward the entrance. Inspector Smivey of Scotland Yard stood there, umbrella tightly rolled, his bowler set square upon his head.

"Who are you?" Willy called out loudly. "We want no interference now."

The inspector merely smiled and walked to the first row of remaining chairs and seated himself comfortably. "Some of you here know me. I am Inspector Smivey of Scotland Yard."

There was a thunder of feet and a concerted rush toward the

exit and the inspector called out loudly, "I wouldn't do that if I were you. There hasn't been an honest workingman on this field for the past half hour. Every man out there, and you will notice that they are pretty much standing about on all sides, is a policeman. Therefore I ask you all to restrain your desires to leave at once and to remain until this present situation is resolved. Do carry on, Hawkin. You were doing quite well until I interrupted."

"But—you said the captain could not possibly be the guilty party."

"So I did, and that is correct. But the rest of your summation has been very accurate and correct up until the last moment. Someone was the originator of the plan, just as you said, and committed all the murders and outrages in the order recited. But I am afraid that your meeting with the captain in Glasgow led you down rather a false trail. Instead of pursuing that lead you should have been following the clue that would have led you to the killer, the clue that was in your possession all the time. The identity of the car the killer escaped from Carradale in."

"That's no good, there is no such number. It was checked by . . . er . . . someone, with the police and the number doesn't exist."

"Very loyal of you. But Miss Ben-Alter contacted me with the number, which was the wisest thing she could do." Cuban, Scot, Egyptian eyes sent glares of hatred in the Israeli direction. Esther smiled at the attention and made a slight curtsy. "If we had had the number and information earlier we could have worked faster, but that is neither here nor there. Suffice to say we were instantly on the job. Firstly, we knew the numbers were false. Easy enough to do in law-abiding Britain where motorists are not obliged to use officially issued number plates but may buy their own, they're sold everywhere. But what kind of a car should this secret master use? A stolen car is too dangerous to drive on an extended trip, too many official eyes see it, officials who have the latest list of missing cars. If it were a privately owned car then, of course, we would not have been able to trace it so easily. But

what if it were a *rented* car." The inspector smiled around, happy
to see his captive audience hanging on his every word. The ten-
sion increased as he stoked an ancient pipe and puffed it to life.

"There you have it. It isn't easy to check every rental car in
Britain for a certain day, but it can be done. There were a number
of Ford Capris out that day, and a certain percentage of them
were green. Not too many though, and by carefully examining
the records we made an astonishing discovery. Remember, very
solid identification must be produced to rent a car costing thou-
sands of pounds, and I'm afraid our master criminal slipped up
on this one point. He rented the car under his own name. Didn't
you Waterbury?"

Tubby blinked and gaped widely, hands jammed in the pockets of the greasy coveralls. "Are you cracked, Inspector? I've
been right here all the time. Maybe someone used my name . . ."

"Sorry. You used your passport and signed your name. Hurried
to Scotland, murdered Angus, grabbed the money, then returned
the same day. We have the mileage on the car and it fits the
trip exactly. Now what do you say to that?"

"Simply this." He took a pistol in a gold-stamped leather holster from his pocket, pulled out the pistol and pointed it at them.
"I have gone through too much to be cheated now. Anyone who
moves will be killed, that's a promise."

Without turning he shuffled backward to the door and fumbled for the release for the emergency exit slide, then pulled it.
Compressed air hissed loudly but, instead of the rubber slide
unfolding, the cover simply flopped open loosely. He reached
inside the container and took out a suitcase.

"The money!" Tony said, stepping forward. The gun swiveled
instantly in his direction.

"Don't be foolish, Tubby," the inspector said calmly. "You
can't get through the cordon of officers below."

"Tubby!" Tubby shrieked. "Tubby and Fatty and Lardy, that's
what they always called me and I always smiled. Old Tubby,
everyone's friend. Always laughing, but now they can laugh out
of the other side of their mouth, oh yes they can. I'm going and

anyone trying to stop me stops a bullet. If your cops try to stop me I kill *her!*"

As he said this he reached out and pulled Esther to him, clumsily with the suitcase in his hand, pressing the gun to her neck.

"Let go of her," Tony called out, taking another step closer.

"Hold it right there, Hawkin, or she gets it, I mean it."

"Sure you do, Tubby," Tony said, attempting a sneer. "Little fat boys are great at beating up on girls."

"Stop, Tony, please," Esther said as she was dragged through the door to the top of the stairs, but he followed right behind.

"Come on, fat stuff. If you're such a big man why don't you shoot *me* instead of a helpless girl? Because if you don't shoot me I'm going to beat about twenty pounds of lard out of your hide."

Tubby Waterbury was shaking with rage, feeling with his feet for the stairs, trying to ignore the insults. But when Tony moved forward suddenly he shouted something wordless, raised the gun and fired. Esther screamed.

Tubby screamed louder as the gun blew up in his hand with a flat thud. His arms flew wide at the shock, Esther dropped to her knees, the bag went flying over the side.

"Are you hurt?" Tony asked Esther, shouldering aside the blubbering, bloody-handed Tubby.

"No, I'm fine, just shocked. You were so brave, for my sake, you shouldn't have done it."

"Well, I wasn't *that* brave. Though I was afraid he might pull the trigger up close and hurt you. That was my gun he had, probably taken from Angus, who took it from Ramon, who took it from me. Or something. I recognized it and remembered it was jimmied to blow up if someone tried to fire it."

"It was still a very brave thing to do and I will love you forever for it."

"*Dyma Cymru!*"

The victorious cry came from the ground below and was followed instantly by the popping sound of a motorbike. The inspector, who already had a cuff on Tubby's good hand and was wrapping a large red kerchief about the bad one, looked up, startled.

Out from under the wing came the stuttering motorbike, ridden by a short white-skinned and dark-haired man. He had the suitcase across the handlebars and as he passed he shook his fist up at them and shouted, "Wales will be free!" then grabbed back at the hand grip and wobbled away rapidly across the field.

"I know that man!" Inspector Smivey roared. "Jones, the chap from Wales Unbound, always after my wife for contributions to the cause because he knows she was born in Swansea." He grated his teeth together. "She's been talking to him, telling him about this case, that's what got him here." He looked at Tony and smiled insincerely. "But we won't mention that will we, Hawkin? He won't get far, I have half the constables in Kent around this field." He extracted a whistle from his pocket and blew a piercing trill. "That'll bring them in. Better round up this lot before we have any more accidents."

FIFTEEN

"All in all a good operation," agent Ross Sones said, shuffling through the papers on his desk, tapping his teeth with his pencil, adjusting his gold-rimmed glasses, smoothing down his bald head. "Started out badly but all's well that ends well, as someone said."

"Shakespeare."

"Who is that, Hawkin, someone else involved with this case you haven't mentioned? There have certainly been some complicated factors, I can see that."

"No, sir, nothing, I think you have it all wrapped up."

"Not exactly all wrapped up. This Scotland Yard man, Smivey, wants a statement from you. Can you get down there this afternoon?"

"Yes, of course, but mention of Scotland Yard brings up one thing that bothers me. Why did you tip them off to arrest me? That's not loyal to the FBI."

"You been drinking too much of this strong beer? I saw a note on your record that you do like to drink, and that can be dangerous. I never blew the whistle on you to the local police."

"Oh no? Then how come after I called you and gave you my phone number two cops showed up at the bar—restaurant—where I was supposed to be waiting?"

"I don't know how the cops showed up, why not ask the cops? Maybe they were thirsty. All I know is I called you back and you weren't there but someone was who tried to sell me an Irish Sweepstake ticket. Why did you leave?"

"But the police *were* looking for me for passing the skyjack bills?"

"Not to my knowledge. If you want to know the truth, and don't word it around, we have not been getting the kind of co-operation here that we normally expect. Well, first it's not their fault, there was difficulty in getting the numbers of the bills over here, the agent with the list was in a plane with engine trouble and he spent a day in Iceland before he could bring the list in. Then the usual thing, who do you give it to? Permission, red tape, the official stamps, the Bank of England getting interested, it's not easy. What with one thing and another we got the numbers to the banks yesterday and today we got the four missing hundred dollar bills in from the banks, and we got them cheap, too, let me tell you, the dollar sort of gliched again and all we had to pay was three hundred and eighty-six bucks. The fourteen dollar profit will look good on the books. Those were the only four missing, the rest were in the bundle the Scotchman had, and in the suitcase—"

"Wait a minute! The police weren't looking for the person who cashed the bills?"

"They are now. If you say you cashed them all that clears up the record and I'll pass the word. I imagine you had good reason. Just to keep the record straight let us say you had four hundred dollars expenses so far on this case, sign this receipt here, and that will close the matter."

Tony signed his name, dazedly, feeling that life had slipped a cog somewhere. "Would you mind telling me just what is happening? The last I saw everyone was being carried away in black marias and I was brought here. Like where is Esther Ben-Alter?"

"In the outside office waiting for you as soon as we are finished. The rest? Let me see the list. The colonel and his pack of counterrevolutionaries. Pretty clear-cut there. They skyjacked the plane and he has been fingered as the man in charge. They'll have a quick trial and will then get filed away in prison for a number of years."

"That's nice. And I know a couple in Glasgow who will be

glad to hear that as well. What about Willy and his Scots patriots?"

"Scotland Yard is sorting that one out, and they're welcome to it. Apparently the only Scotchman they can prove was involved physically in the skyjacking was Angus, now deceased. They are trying to find out which of the other Scots were involved in the affair, but it's difficult, they are a closed-mouth lot, not very friendly."

"Longest occupied country in the history of the world."

"I'm sure that has something to do with it. But we're not involved in that part of the business, thank goodness, though Scotland Yard wants you to try and identify any of the men who took the money from the car."

"That's going to be hard," Tony said, in a burst of Highland loyalty. "Scotchmen are like Indians, hard to tell one from the other."

"You're probably right. Just tell them what you know and sign the affidavit. Who else? They have that Egyptian girl as an accomplice, as well as some Al Fatah thug they picked up trying to slip out of the country."

"Justice will be done."

"That's about it. A good roundup of all involved, some quick trials and open and shut convictions, all the money returned. Here's your passport, you never did pick it up. I've booked you on a late flight tomorrow."

"Wait a minute! I have to go to Scotland Yard, make depositions, get a shave, lots of things. Is there any reason I can't stay on here a bit—they can take it off my vacation time?"

"There have been a couple of flaps back at your operation, I understand. Something about chocolate hand grenades."

"They can last without me a few days more. Come on, Sones buddy, be a buddy, will you? We've been through thick and thin together, Mexico and England, Washington and, you know, everything. Make some excuses, get me a week. I'll pay for it myself, really I will."

Sones chewed the inside of his cheek meditatively. "Well—

don't see why not. They may need you here for questioning, have that Inspector Smivey report that officially and you'll have a reason. Do you think he'll co-operate?"

"I know he will." Memories of the Free Wales movement glowed brightly before him. "I'll have that letter for you today."

"Then that about wipes it up, Hawkin. I'm going back tonight with the money, special Air Force plane and armed guard, taking no chances. I'll put my report in when I get back. This will look good on your record, yes it will. I can tell you now, in all confidence, I was never really sure of you after that last operation in Mexico. But you're a trouper, Hawkin, a credit to the Bureau. Too bad you're not a better shot. Close the door behind you on the way out."

He had to open the door first to do this, and when he did he came face to face with Stocker, the burly Treasury agent. The fact that Stocker was carrying a large and familiar suitcase did not interfere with his reflexes, so that with an incredibly swift movement he produced a sawed-off submachine gun and leveled it at Tony.

"Easy," Tony called out, stepping back. "Would you please watch the artillery. Aren't you forgetting that I'm the one who recovered that money for you?"

Grudgingly, Stocker returned the gun to one of his bulging pockets, bulging with weapons as Tony well knew, and scowled a mean scowl in Tony's direction.

"Ahh know about that, but it was long enough bein' done. And some of the bills 'r soiled, got writin' on them . . ."

"Come on, Stocker, they're still worth the same amount. Haven't you got one nice word about how we recovered the money?"

Apparently he hadn't for he stalked on by without even a friendly grunt, followed closely by two of his eagle-eyed colleagues. Tony stood aside to let them pass, then went on into the outer office where Esther was waiting, looking out of the window at the green trees in Grosvenor Square that partially obscured the statue of F.D.R. She turned quickly when Tony came out.

"You're going home," she said, her voice carefully emotionless.

"Soon. But I would like to ask you a question or two if you don't mind."

"I have been waiting for those questions." She lowered her eyes.

"You knew all along that the police didn't want me for passing those bills. In fact it looks like you were working hand in glove with the police. Why didn't you tell me?"

"I wanted to, believe me. But the inspector insisted that you be allowed to go on in your own way. You were doing so well and were so deeply involved with the skyjackers that you did a better job of uncovering everything than anyone else could possibly have done. It was important to us, you must understand that. The police have not been all that kind to us here and it helped to co-operate with them to uncover the truth in this skyjacking affair. We take no credit, but they know we co-operated. They won't bother us as much in the future. Please understand, I had such divided loyalties. What else could I do? I did want to tell you and . . ."

She turned away and pressed a small handkerchief to her face. He turned her back again and carefully kissed each salty eye.

"I don't blame you in the slightest. As that well-known Shakesperian scholar Ross Sones says, 'All's well that ends well.' And I'm not going right away. I may have as much as a whole week. Would you like to show me some of the sights of the city?"

"Would I!" She laughed. "There's the Tower of London, British Museum . . ."

"Art museums are more in my line. Would you mind?"

"I'd love it. In fact there is an exhibition of Cuban revolutionary posters right now at the Royal Academy . . ."

"Later perhaps, much later. First something safely in the sixteenth century, then we sneak up on the twentieth ever so slowly. Then dinner after. All right with you?"

"Couldn't be better, I agree completely."

Arm in arm, laughing, they went down the stairs together and out into the pellucid joy of a London spring. Attenuated fallout from French atomic bombs filtered down around them, an overly expensive Concord supersonic airship thundered invisibly high above them, in distant places men of many colors fired weapons in anger at one another but, for the moment, they were unaware of this.

The door of a pub yawned invitingly and they entered, still laughing, eager to see what joys the future days would bring.